LITTLE MOUNTAIN

Emergent Literatures

LITTLE
MOUNTAIN

Elias KHOURY

Translation by Maia TABET

Foreword by
Edward W. SAID

UNIVERSITY of MINNESOTA PRESS, Minneapolis

Published by the University of Minnesota Press
2037 University Avenue Southeast, Minneapolis MN 55414.
Printed in the United States of America.

The Koranic quotation on p. 133, Chapter 5, is Chapter XXVII, "The
Ant," verse 34, and was taken from A. J. Arberry, *The Koran Inter-
preted*, George Allen Unwin Ltd, 1965.

Library of Congress Cataloging-in-Publication Data

Khūrī, Ilyās.
    [Jabal al-ṣaghīr. English]
    Little mountain / Elias Khoury ; translation by Maia Tabet.
      p.   cm. —(Emergent literatures)
    Translation of: al-Jabal al-ṣaghīr.
    ISBN 0-8166-1769-4   ISBN 0-8166-1770-8 (pbk.)
    I. Title.   II. Series.
PJ7842.H823J3413   1989
892'.736—dc20   89-31940
                                            CIP

To the memory of
Mohammad Shbaro and his companions

Contents

Foreword

Edward W. SAID

The first English translation of Elias Khoury's novel *Little Mountain* needs to be set in the context of the Arabic novel, from which, in equal measure, it derives and departs. As a contemporary Lebanese writer, Khoury embodies the curious and tragic dialectics between his country and its surrounding environment, recently thrust into literary prominence by the 1988 Nobel Prize for Literature.

Naguib Mahfouz's achievement as the greatest living Arab novelist and first Arab winner of the Nobel Prize has in small but significant measure now retrospectively vindicated his unmatched regional reputation, and belatedly given him recognition in the West. For of all the major literatures and languages, Arabic is by far the least known and the most grudgingly regarded by Europeans and Americans, a huge irony given that all Arabs regard the immense literary and cultural worth of their language as one of their principal contributions to the world. Arabic is of course the language of the Koran and is therefore central to Islam, in which it has a hieratic, historical, and everyday use that is almost without parallel in other world cultures. Because of that role, and because it has always been associated with resistance to the imperialist incursions that have characterized Arab history since the late eighteenth century, Arabic has also acquired a uniquely disputatious position in modern culture, defended and extolled by its native speakers and writers, belittled, attacked, or ignored by foreigners for whom it has represented a last defended bastion of Arabism and Islam.

During the 130 years of French colonialism in Algeria, for example, Arabic was effectively proscribed as a quotidian language; to a lesser degree, the same was roughly true in Tunisia and Morocco, in which an uneasy bilingualism arose because the French language was politically imposed on the native Arabs. Elsewhere in the Arab *mashriq* Arabic became the focus of hopes for reform and renaissance, and as Benedict Anderson has discussed the matter in *Imagined Communities*, the spread of literacy spurred the rise of modern nationalism, in the midst of which narrative prose fiction played a crucial role in creating a national consciousness. By providing readers not only with a sense of their common past—for example in the historical romances of the early twentieth-century novelist and historian Jurji Zaydan—but also with a sense of an abiding communal continuity, Arabic novelists stood squarely wherever issues of destiny, society, and direction were being debated or investigated.

We should not forget, however, that the novel as it is known in the West is a relatively new form in the rich Arabic literary tradition. And along with that we should keep in mind that as it develops mainly in the twentieth century the Arabic novel is an engaged form, involved through its readers and authors in the great social and historical upheavals of our century, sharing in triumphs as well as failures. Thus, to return to Mahfouz and to connect what I have been saying with his particular situation as he was accorded the 1988 Nobel Prize, his work from the late 1930s on compresses the history of the European novel into a relatively short span of time. He is thus not only a Hugo and a Dickens, but also a Galsworthy, a Mann, Zola, and Jules Romain. In addition — as the almost comic consternation followed by journalistic silence that attended on the Stockholm announcement attests — his work is scarcely known in the West. Seven or eight of his novels in barely serviceable translations are available in English, none of them in currency or a part of normal literacy. It is perhaps worth adding as a pendant to the eccentricity of this Scandinavian episode, that a few years ago when I was asked by a major New York publisher to recommend some Third World fiction titles for translation, Mahfouz was at the top of my list. When my recommendation was turned down, the publisher offered by way of only slightly embarrassed explanation the rueful observation that "Arabic after all is a controversial language."

Surrounded therefore by politics, and to a very great degree caught up in the contests of the native as well as the international environment, the Arabic novel is truly an embattled form. Mahfouz's allegorical novel, *Awlad Haritna* (1959), also takes on Islam and was banned in Egypt when it was about to be published in book form (it had already appeared in serial form). His earlier Cairo *Trilogy* (1956-57) traversed the phases of Egyptian nationalism culminating in the 1952 Revolution, and did so critically and yet intimately as a participant in the remaking of Egyptian society with it. *Miramar* (1967), his Rashomon-style novel about Alexandria, puts a sour face on Nasser's socialism, its abuses, anomalies, and human costs. During the late 1960s his short stories and novels addressed the aftermath of the 1967 war, sympathetically in the case of an emergent Palestinian resistance, critically in the case of Egyptian military intervention in Yemen. Mahfouz was the most celebrated writer and cultural figure to greet the Egyptian-Israeli peace treaty in 1979, and although his books were banned in Arab countries for a time after that, his stature was too solidly great to be diminished for long. Even in Egypt the position he took was apparently unpopular, yet he has not only survived the temporary opprobrium but has emerged (if anything) more august and admired.

Mahfouz's career is of course distinguished in the Arab world, not only because of the extraordinary length of his writing life, but also because his work is so thoroughly Egyptian (and Cairene), based as it is on a territorial and imaginative vision of a society unique in the Middle East. The thing about Mahfouz is that he can and has always been able to depend on the vital integrity and even, cultural compactness of Egypt. For all its tremendous age, the variety of its components and the influences on it—the merest listing of these is inhibitingly impressive: Pharonic, Arab, Muslim, Hellenistic, European, Christian, Judiac, etc.—the country has a stability and identity that in this century have not disappeared. Put differently, this is to say that the Arabic novel has flourished especially well in twentieth-century Egypt because throughout all the turbulence of the country's wars, revolutions, and social upheavals, civil society was never eclipsed, its existence was never in doubt, was never completely absorbed into the State. Novelists like Mahfouz had it always *there* for them, and accordingly developed an abiding institutional connection with the society through their fiction.

Moreover, the historical and geographical topography of the Cairo mapped by Mahfouz has been handed down to the generation of writers who came to maturity in the post-1952 period. Gamal al-Ghitany is like Mahfouz, in that several of his works are set in Fatimid Cairo (for example, his recently translated *Zayni Barakat*) in districts like

Gamaliyia, which is where Mahfouz's realistic work of 1947, *Midaq Alley*, is also set. Ghitany considers himself one of Mahfouz's heirs, so that the overlap in setting and treatment confirms the generational relationship between older and younger man, made easier and dependable through the city of Cairo and Egyptian identity. To later generations of Egyptian writers then, Mahfouz's precedence assures them of a point of departure, just as for Dickens, the work of Fielding, Defoe, and Smollett had established the discursive patterns of a narrative structure that was not merely a passive reflection of an evolving society, but an organic part of it.

Yet Mahfouz as, so to speak, patron and progenitor of subsequent Egyptian fiction is not by any means a provincial writer, nor simply a local influence. Here another discrepancy is important and worth noting. Because of its size and power, Egypt has always been a locus for Arab ideas and movements; in addition Cairo has functioned as a diffusionary center for print publishing, films, radio, and television. Arabs in Morocco, on the one hand, Iraq, on the other, who may have very little in common are likely to have had a lifetime of watching Egyptian films (or television serials) to connect them. Similarly, modern Arabic literature has spread out from Cairo for the whole of our century; for years Mahfouz was a resident writer at *al-Ahram*, Egypt's leading daily. Mahfouz's novels, his characters and concerns, have been the privileged, if not always emulated, norm for most other Arab novelists, at the very same moment that Arabic literature as a whole has remained marginal to Western readers for whom Fuentes, Garcia Marquez, Soyinka, and Rushdie have acquired vital cultural authority.

What I have sketched so schematically is something of the background assumed when a contemporary, non-

Egyptian writer of substantial gifts wishes to write fiction in Arabic. To speak of an "anxiety of influence," so far as the precedence of Mahfouz, Egypt, and Europe (which is where in effect the Arabic novel before Mahfouz came from) are concerned, is to speak of something socially and politically actual. Anxiety is at work not only about what in so fundamentally settled and integral a society as Egypt was possible for a Mahfouz, but also about what in a fractured, decentered, and openly insurrectionary place is maddeningly, frustratingly *not* possible. For one, in some Arab countries you cannot leave your house and suppose that when and if you return it will be as you left it. For another, you can no longer take for granted that such places as hospitals, schools, and government buildings will function as they do elsewhere, or if they do for a while, that they will continue to do so next week. For a third, you cannot be certain that such recorded, certified, and registered stabilities in all societies—birth, marriage, death—will in fact be noted or in any way commemorated. Rather, most aspects of life are negotiable, not just with money and normal social intercourse, but also with guns and rocket-propelled-grenades (RPG's).

The extreme cases in which such eventualities are daily occurrences are Palestine and Lebanon, the first a state that simply stopped existing in 1948, the second a country that began its public self-destruction in April 1975, and has not stopped. Yet in both polities there are and have been Lebanese as well as Palestinian people, for whom their national identity is threatened with extinction (the latter) or with daily dissolution (the former). In such societies the novel is both a risky and highly problematic form. Typically its subjects are urgently political, and its concerns radically existential. Literature in stable societies (Egypt's, for instance) is only replicable by Palestinian and Lebanese writers by means of parody and exaggeration, since on a minute-by-minute basis social life for Lebanese and Palestinian writers is an enterprise with highly unpredictable results. And above all, form is an adventure, narrative both uncertain and meandering, character less a stable collection of traits than a linguistic device, as self-conscious as it is provisional and ironic.

Take first two Palestinian novelists, Ghassan Kanafani and Emile Habibi. Kanafani's seems at first sight the more conventional mode, Habibi's the wildly experimental. Yet even in *Rijal fil Shams* (Men in the Sun, 1963) Kanafani's story of Palestinian loss and death is undermined as a narrative by the novel's peculiarly disintegrating prose, in which within a group of two or three sentences time and place are in so relentlessly constant a state of flux that the reader is never absolutely certain where and when the story is taking place. In his most complex long narrative *Ma Tabaqqa Lakum* (What is Left for You, 1966) this technique is even more pronounced, so that even in one short paragraph multiple narrators speak without, so far as the reader is concerned, adequate markers, distinctions, delimitations. And yet so definitely pronounced is the unhappy fate of the Palestinian characters depicted by Kanafani that a kind of aesthetic clarification, by which story, character, and fate come jarringly together, occurs in their terrible encounter with it. In the earlier work the three refugees are asphyxiated in a tanker-truck on the Iraqi-Kuwaiti border, in the later novel Mariam stabs her abusive and bigamous husband while her brother Hamid faces an Israeli in a mortal encounter.

Habibi's *Pessoptimist* (1974) is a carnivalesque explosion of parody and theatrical farce, continuously surprising, shocking, unpredictable. It makes no concessions at all to any of the standard fictional conventions. Its main character (whose name jams together Pessimism and Optimism) is an amalgam of something out of Aesop, al-Hariri, Kafka, Dumas, and Walt Disney, its action a combination of low political farce, science fiction, adventure, and Biblical prophecy, all of it anchored in the restless dialectic of Habibi's semi-colloquial, semi-classical prose. Whereas Kanafani's occasional, but affecting melodramatic touches put him within reach of Mahfouz's novels in their disciplined and situated action, Habibi's world is Rabelais and even Joyce to the Egyptian's Balzac and Galsworthy. It is as if the Palestinian situation now in its fifth decade without resolution produces a wildly erratic and free-wheeling version of the picaresque novel, which in its flaunting of its carelessness and spite is in Arabic prose fiction about as far as one can get from Mahfouz's stateliness.

Lebanon, the other recently eccentric and resistant society, has been rendered most typically in language not by novels or even stories, but by far more ephemeral forms—journalism, popular songs, cabaret parody, essays. So powerful in its disintegrating effects has been the Civil War which officially began in April 1975 that readers of Lebanese writing need an occasional reminder that this after all is (or was) an Arabic country, whose language and heritage share a great deal with writers like Mahfouz. Indeed in Lebanon the novel exists largely as a form recording its own impossibility, shading off or breaking into autobiography (as in the remarkable proliferation of Lebanese women's writing), reportage, pastiche, or apparently authorless discourse.

Thus at the other limit from Mahfouz we can disengage the politically committed and, in its own highly mobile modes, brilliant figure of Elias Khoury whose earliest important work of fiction, *Little Mountain* (1977), now appears in English for the first time. Khoury is a mass of paradoxes, especially when compared with other Arab novelists of his generation. Like Ghitany he is, and has been for at least twelve years, a practicing journalist; at present he edits the weekly cultural page of the Leftist Beirut daily *As-Safir*. Unlike Ghitany—whose gifts for invention and sheer verbal bravura he shares—Khoury was from his early days an actively engaged militant, having grown up as a 1960s schoolboy in the turbulent world of Lebanese and Palestinian street politics. Some of the scenes of the city and mountain fighting during the early (autumn 1975 and early 1976) days of the Lebanese Civil War described in *Little Mountain* are based on these experiences. Also unlike Ghitany, Khoury is a publishing-house editor, having worked for a leading Beirut publisher for a decade during which he established an impressive list of Arabic translations of major postmodern Third World classics (Fuentes, Marquez, Asturias, etc.).

Nor is this all. Khoury is a highly perceptive critic, associated with the avant-garde poet Adonis, and his (now defunct) Beirut quarterly *Mawaqif*. Between them members of the *Mawaqif* group were responsible during the 1970s for some of the most searching investigations of modernity and modernism as applied to Arab culture; as explicator, critic, polemicist, translator, and formulator of new ideas, Khoury came to remarkable prominence while still in his 20s. It is out of this work, along with his engaged journalism—almost alone among Christian Lebanese writers he espoused the cause of resistance to the Israeli occupation of South Lebanon (see his book *Zaman al-Ihtilal*, *Period of Occupation*) and did so publicly and relentlessly at great personal risk from the heart of West Beirut—fiction, editing, translating, and literary criticism that Khoury has forged (in the Joycean sense) a national and novel, unconventional, fundamentally postmodern literary career.

This is in stark contrast to Mahfouz, whose Flaubertian dedication to letters has followed a more or less modernist trajectory. Khoury's ideas about literature and society are of a piece with the often bewilderingly fragmented realities of Lebanon in which, he says in one of his essays, the past is discredited, the future completely uncertain, the present unknowable. For him perhaps the most symptomatic and yet the finest strand of modern Arabic writing derives not from the stable and highly replicable forms originally native to the Arabic tradition (the *qasidah*) or imported from the West (the novel) but those works he calls formless—e.g., Tawfik al-Hakim's *Diaries of a Country Lawyer*, Taha Hussein's *Stream of Days*, Gibran's and Nuaimah's writings. These works, Khoury says, are profoundly attractive and have in fact created the "new" Arabic writing which cannot be found in the more traditional fictions produced by conventional novelists. What Khoury finds in these formless works is precisely what Western theorists have called postmodern: that combinatorial amalgam of different elements, principally autobiography, story, fable, pastiche, and self-parody, the whole highlighted by an insistent and eerie nostalgia.

Little Mountain replicates in its own special brand of formlessness some of Khoury's life: his early years in Ashrafiyyeh (Christian East Beirut, also known as the Little Mountain), his exile from it for having taken a stand with the nationalist (Muslim and Palestinian forces) coalition, subsequent military campaigns during the latter part of 1975—in downtown Beirut and the eastern mountains of Lebanon—and finally an exilic encounter with a friend in Paris. The work's five chapters thus exfoliate outward from the family house in Ashrafiyyeh, to which neither Khoury nor the narrator can return given the irreversible dynamics of the Lebanese Civil Wars, and when the chapters conclude, they come to no rest, no final cadence, no respite. For indeed Khoury's prescience in this work of 1977 was to have forecast a worsening of the situation, in which Lebanon's modern(ist) history was terminated, and from which a string of almost unimaginable disasters (the massacres, the Syrian and Israeli interventions, the current political impasse with partition already in place) have followed.

Style in *Little Mountain* is, first of all, repetition, as if the narrator needed reiteration to prove to himself that improbable things actually *did* take place. Repetition is also, as the narrator says, the search for order—to go over matters sufficiently to find, if possible, the underlying pattern, the rules and protocols according to which the Civil War, most dreaded of all social calamities, is being fought. Repetition permits lyricism, those metaphorical flights by which the sheer horror of what takes place ("Ever since the Mongols . . . we've been dying like flies. Dying without thinking. Dying of disease, of bilharzia, of the plague. . . . Without any consciousness, without dignity, without anything.") is swiftly seen and recorded, and then falls back into indistinct anonymity.

Style for Khoury is also comedy and irreverence. For how else is one to apprehend those religious verities for which one fights—the truth of Christianity, for instance—if churches are also soldiers' camps, and if priests like the French Father Marcel in Chapter Two of *Little Mountain*, are garrulous and inebriated racists? Khoury's picaresque ramblings through the Lebanese landscapes offered by civil combat reveal areas of uncertainty and perturbation unthought of before, whether in the tranquility of childhood or in the certainties provided by primordial sect, class, or family. What emerges finally is not the well-shaped, studied forms sculpted by an artist (like Mahfouz) of the *mot juste*, but a series of zones swept by half-articulated anxi-

eties, memories, and unfinished action. Occasionally a pre-
ternatural clarity is afforded us, usually in the form of
nihilistic aphorisms ("The men of learning discovered that
they too could loot"), or of beach scenes, but the disorien-
tation is almost constant.

In Khoury's writing therefore we get an extraordinary sensation of *informality* persuaded gently and not
always successfully through the channels of narrative. Thus
the story of an unraveling society is put before us as the narrator is forced to leave home, fights through the streets of
Beirut and up into the mountains, experiences the death of
comrades and of love, ends up accosted by a disturbed vet-
eran in the corridors and on the platform of the Paris metro.
The startling originality of *Little Mountain* is its avoidance
of the melodramatic and the conventional; Khoury plots ep-
isodes without illusion or foreseeable pattern, much as a
suddenly released extraterrestrial prisoner might wander
from place to place, backward and forward, taking things in
through a surprisingly well-articulated earth-language,
which is always approximate and somehow embarrassing to
him.

Finally of course Khoury's work embodies the very
actuality of Lebanon's predicament, so unlike Egypt's ma-
jestic stability as delivered in Mahfouz's fiction. I suspect,
however, that Khoury's is actually a more typical version of
reality, at least so far as the present course of the Middle
East is concerned. Novels have always been tied to national
states, but in the Arab world the modern state has been de-
rived from the experience of colonialism, imposed from
above and handed down, rather than earned through the
travails of independence. It is no indictment of Mahfouz's
enormous achievement to say that of the opportunities offered the Arab writer during the twentieth century his has
been conventional in the honorable sense: he took the novel

from Europe and fashioned it according to Egypt's Muslim and Arab identity, quarreling and arguing with the Egyptian state, but finally, always, and already its citizen. Khoury's achievement is at the other end of the scale. Orphaned by history, he is the minority Christian whose fate has become nomadic because it cannot accommodate itself to the Christian exclusionism and xenophobia shared by other minorities in the region. The underlying aesthetic form of his experience is assimilation—since he remains an Arab, very much part of the culture—infected by rejection, drift, errance, uncertainty. Yet Khoury's writing represents the difficult days of search and experiment now expressed in the Arab East by the Palestinian *intifadah*, as newly released energies push through the set repositories of habit and national life and burst into terrible civil disturbance. Khoury, along with Mahmoud Darwish, is an artist giving voice to rooted exiles and trapped refugees, to dissolving boundaries and changing identities, to radical demands and new languages. From this perspective Khoury's work bids Mahfouz an inevitable and yet profoundly respectful farewell.

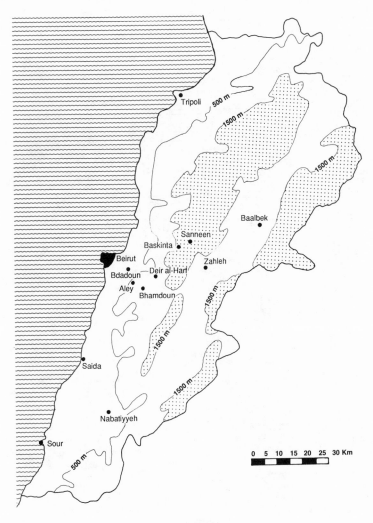

Tripoli

500 m

1500 m

1500 m

Baalbek

Sanneen

Baskinta

Beirut

Zahleh

Deir al-Harf

Bdadoun

Aley

Bhamdoun

1500 m

1500 m

Saida

1500 m

Nabatiyyeh

Sour

500 m

0 5 10 15 20 25 30 Km

LEBANON

LITTLE MOUNTAIN   xxiii

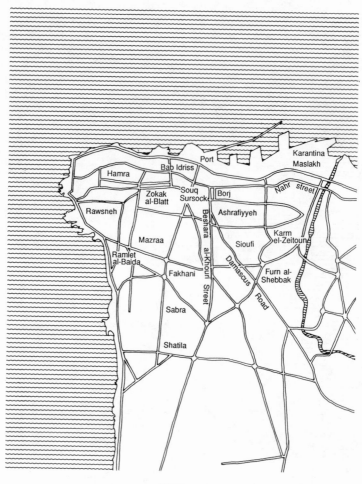

BEIRUT

Elias KHOURY

LITTLE
MOUNTAIN

Chapter 1

LITTLE MOUNTAIN

They call it Little Mountain.* And we called it Little Mountain. We'd carry pebbles, draw faces and look for a puddle of water to wash off the sand, or fill with sand, then cry. We'd run through the fields—or something like fields—pick up a tortoise and carry it to where green leaves littered the ground. We made up things we'd say or wouldn't say. They call it Little Mountain, we knew it wasn't a mountain and we called it Little Mountain.

One hill, several hills, I no longer remember and no one remembers anymore. A hill on Beirut's eastern flank which we called mountain because the mountains were far away. We sat on its slopes and stole the sea. The sun rose in the East and we'd come out of the wheatfields from the East. We'd pluck off the ears of wheat, one by one, to amuse ourselves. The poor—or what might have been the poor—skipped through the fields on the hills, like children, questioning Nature about Her things. What we called a *'eid*** was a day like any other, but it was laced with the smell of the *burghul* and *'araq*† that we ate in Nature's world, tell-

---

* The popular name for the Ashrafiyyeh area of Beirut.
** That is, a feast day, festival, or holiday of religious origin or significance.
† *Burghul* is the crushed wheat used in two major national dishes in Lebanon; it is known in the West as bulgar. *'Araq*, the national drink, is a distilled grape alcohol, aromatized with anis.

ing it about our world which subsists in our memory like a dream. Little Mountain was just a tip of rock we'd steal into, wonderous and proud. We'd spin yarns about our miseries awaiting the moments of joy or death, dallying with our feelings to break the monotony of the days.

They call it Little Mountain. It stretched across the vast fields dotted with prickly-pear bushes. The palm tree in front of our house was bent under the weight of its own trunk. We were afraid it would brush the ground, crash down to it, so we suggested tying it with silken rope to the window of our house. But the house itself, with its thick sandstone and wooden ceilings, was caving in and we got frightened the palm tree would bring the house down with it. So we let it lean farther day by day. And every day I'd embrace its fissured trunk and draw pictures of my face on it.

We feared for the mountain and for its plants. It edged to the brink of Beirut, sinking into it. And the prickly-pear bushes that scratched our legs were dying and the palm tree leaning and the mountain edging toward the brink.

They call it Little Mountain. We knew it wasn't a mountain and we called it Little Mountain.

* * *

Five men come, jumping out of a military-like jeep. Carrying automatic rifles, they surround the house. The neighbors come out to watch. One of them smiles, she makes the victory sign. They come up to the house, knock on the door. My mother opens the door, suprised. Their leader asks about me.

—He's gone out.
—Where did he go?

—I don't know.

—Come in, have a cup of coffee.

They enter. They search for me in the house. I wasn't there. They search the books and the papers. I wasn't there. They found a book with a picture of Abdel-Nasser* on the back cover. I wasn't there. They scattered the papers and overturned the furniture. They cursed the Palestinians. They ripped my bed up. They insulted my mother and this corrupt generation. I wasn't there. I wasn't there. My mother was there, trembling with distress and resentment, pacing up and down the house angrily. She stopped answering their questions and left them. She sat on a chair in the entrance, guarding her house as they, inside, looked for the Palestinians and Abdel-Nasser and international communism. She sat on a chair in the entrance, guarding her house as they, inside, tore up papers and memories. She sat on a chair and they made the sign of the cross, in hatred or in joy.

They went out into the street, their hands held high in gestures of victory. Some people watched and made the victory sign.

* * *

We called it Little Mountain when we were small. We'd run along its dirt roads or on the edge of the asphalt which cut into our feet. We'd walk its streets looking for things to play with. And during the holidays, I'd go with my father and brothers to the fields called Sioufi and frolic between the olive and Persian lilac trees. There, we'd stand on top of a high hill overlooking three roads: the Nahr Beirut road, the Karm al-Zeytoun road** and the third one, which we called the road to our house. We'd stand on the high

---

* The president of Egypt from 1954 to 1970 and the most revered leader of Arab Nationalism.

** That is, the Beirut River and Olive Grove roads, respectively.

open hilltop, run through it and always be afraid of falling off onto one of the three roads.

He stood perched on the high hill. Holding his big father by the right hand, he'd watch the cars far away on the road below and marvel at how small they were. They weren't like the car he rode to his uncle's distant house. Very small cars, one behind the other, like the small car that his father bought him and set in motion by singing to it. There's not a sound to these metal cars going by. Soundless, they move along regularly, one behind the other, in a straight line. They don't stop. Inside are miniature-like people. They aren't children of my age — he'd think to himself — and once, when he asked his father about the secret of the small cars, his father answered in the overtones of a diviner that the reason was that Ashrafiyyeh being a mountain, the Beirutis went and spent the summer there. And compared with Beirut, the mountain is high. The distance between us and the Nahr Beirut is high, like that between us and the Karm al-Zeytoun road. And the farther you are, the smaller things get. Later, when you grow up, you'll see that the cars are very small. Because vision is also related to the size of the viewer. I would nod, feigning comprehension, not under-standing a thing. Generally, I'd let my father tell me his story, which he always retold, about distances and cars and distract myself by chasing a golden cicada flitting among the green grasses or perched between the branches of the olive trees.

A long line of small soundless cars. We'd sit on the edge of the hill and watch them go by, waiting for the day when we'd grow up and see that they were very small really, or go down to the road and see that they were very big. They trickled by like colored drops of water of varying size. Trucks, petrol tankers, all sorts of small cars. We could tell the difference between them although we couldn't name them or say what they were for. They were far away and small and we'd hold each other by the hand waiting to grow up so they'd grow even smaller, we'd hold each other by the hand and wait to understand the secret. And I always used to wonder how come cars were small just because they were far away and I would daydream about the stories of dwarfs they told us at school or of the man whom the devil turned into a dwarf, which my grandmother always told me.

Little Mountain where it was, the vegetation that covered its handsome mound was giving way to roads and we rejoiced at the opening of the first cinema in Sioufi. But surprises awaited me. We were growing and what we had been waiting for, so long now, didn't happen. We were getting bigger, we'd go to Sioufi to watch the cars—and see that they'd gotten bigger. We got bigger and the cars got bigger. Hemmed in by the gathering clamor and frenzy. We were getting bigger and the once-straight lines were curving, the clamor getting closer and the spaces narrower. I walk alone, Little Mountain twists and turns. I search for memories of when Palm Sunday* was a 'eid and we came out of the church to the sound of Eastern chants: I find only a small, neglected picture in my pocket.

Cars growing, closing in on me. Trees shrinking, disappearing. I was growing bigger and so were the cars, around my neck were their sounds, their colors, their sizes. Now, we can tell the difference between them but we don't understand.

Old expectations and distant memories are merely expectations and memories. At night, the cars climb the three roads to the high hilltop. Bruising my eyes, their lights encircle me. The whine of the engines walling me in as they approach my face. The cars are big, they have huge

---

* In the Eastern church, Palm Sunday is an important festival especially for children.

eyes extending filaments of fire that don't burn. They leave the traces of terror, of questions and answers, on my face.

The cars were growing—and we were growing. The broad streets were growing and the trees bent low on Little Mountain. What has become of my father's explanations as he told me stories of distance and height and size?

You stand alone amid the flood of lights that blinds you and robs you of your memory. You go looking for your house, alone, memoryless.

* * *

Abu George told me the story of the names. Abu George has been my friend since the time I wandered around Little Mountain, alone among the lights, looking for my father's explanations. He'd find me alone, sitting on the edge of a hill overlooking the railroad tracks of the slow train that stands out in my memory, and would tell me his stories of the French and the world war.

He'd relate how Sioufi used to be a huge property owned by a man called Yusef as-Sagheer.* That is why Ashrafiyyeh was called Little Mountain. Then, the brothers Elias and Nkoula Sioufi bought it up dirt-cheap and, after World War I, they built a furniture factory on it. The neighborhood came to be known by their name.

The factory, in reality a large workshop, was an event in itself. It had about fifty workers. They built themselves some shacks nearby, and a small café serving coffee and 'araq opened next door. The factory was a novel sort of undertaking and people began getting used to a novel way of life, for the first time. Modern machines. European-style furniture. They knew neither where it went nor how it would be sold. They collected their wage—or something like a wage—at the end of the month, gave some of it to their women, and drank 'araq with the rest.

* As-Sagheer means the little one in Arabic.

As the neighborhood got used to this new kind of life, there arose a new kind of theft. Instead of the old kind of robberies—like those of a man called Nadra who lived at the eastern end of the neighborhood and who, in the ancient Arab tradition of chivalry, extorted money from the rich to give it to the poor—there was now organized robbery. Gang robbery, premeditated and merciless; without a touch of chivalry or any other kind of principle. The most important event which established this new-style thieving was the robbery of the Sioufi factory itself. At the end of each month, the accountant would go to Beirut to fetch the workers' money and come back to the factory to distribute it to them. Once, at a crossroads, some thieves ambushed him; they took the money and left him there, hollering. Alerted by his screams, the workers gathered around. Men, women, and children rushed out and chased the thieves. The thieves ran and people ran behind them, popping out of the dirt roads and alleys. Before anyone had caught up with them, the thieves stopped running, threw the coins to the ground and resumed their race. At that point, bodies doubled up over coins and hands started snatching. People forgot the thieves and let them get away, snatching up the coins from the ground helter-skelter. It was no chivalrous kind of theft, Abu George would say. Why? Because they all forgot their honor and made for the coins. They were lenient with the thieves and took the factory's money. That is when the decline set it. And the story has it, the factory started going bankrupt then, Abu George would continue. Elias Sioufi died of a broken heart and his brother, Nkoula, sold off the property to the people of the neighborhood. And it was split into small holdings.

However, Abu George went on, there was perhaps another reason for the bankruptcy. People who knew Nkoula Sioufi—who had become an errand-runner at the

Ministry of Finance—said the reason was that he drank and gambled and associated with foreigners. God only knows, Abu George would say. But the decline set in with the beginning of this new-style thieving. And we now have to deal with things we never knew.

* * *

Is the mountain slipping?

The big cars advanced, invading, their whine filling the streets. The mountain was being penetrated from all sides. They cut the trees, erected buildings. The concrete mountain's machines were everywhere. In every street, there was a machine, Syrian and Kurdish workers swarming around it, throwing sand, gravel and water into its entrails. Rotating on itself, spilling out the cement used to build the tall, indomitable buildings. Buildings shot up as though born here and the thick, warm sandstone tumbled to the ground and was replaced by the hollow, cold cement blocks. And the wheel turned. Hundreds of workers came up here from the tin shacks clustered at the eastern entrance of Beirut—called Qarantina*—to carry gravel and sand and spread the cement across the squares.

Bulldozers came, flattening the hills to the ground or what was presumed to be the level of the ground. And in front of our house, the palm tree collapsed, locked into the excavator's jaws, its roots which bulged above ground, torn out and cast down, in a pool of gravel and sand. Torn like small arteries by a bombshell. The new buildings soared. Mountains of buildings, roads and squares.

Is the mountain slipping?

I walk its side streets, looking for my childhood. Before me on the hill which I call mountain, a gentle slope

---

* The area known as Qarantina was the site of a military quarantine hospital under the French Mandate. Later, it became Beirut's principal garbage dump and part of the urban slum area that constituted the city's "belt of misery." (See note on p. 28.)

separating the mountain from Nahr Beirut. The small cars have grown and I have grown. And the tall buildings now hide the sea. I used to think we had stolen the sea. But the smell of reinforced concrete has stolen the smell of the sea.

The mountain isn't slipping.

The hubbub at its gates, the buildings multiplying and the squares being built. That loud voice is no longer mine. Noise cowering at the gates and frenzy the new sign. This is Little Mountain which isn't slipping.

Concrete soaring and heads soaring. Heavy music soaring and heads soaring. On my body, I bear from those days an ancient tattoo and I wait, on the brink.

1956: the tripartite attack on Egypt. We were at the poor, small neighborhood school. We were little. We'd listen to *Sawt al-Arab*.* We went home and rejoiced when Egypt won.

1958: barricades in the neighborhood. Somber faces. The Muslims want to kill us. My mother didn't believe it. She always said that's crazy. They're very much like us.

The tall buildings have become barricades. Things have changed. The gathering clamor. Things have changed. The cars are growing and we are growing.

* * *

Abu George would go on with his story about the furniture factory. He'd never weary of recounting his memories of the neighborhood, considering himself a part of its history. And at every turn, he'd ponder with me the use of living. He'd talk at length of how his brother was a soldier with the French army in Hawran,** of how he rebelled

---

* The Cairo-based pan-Arab radio listened to extensively throughout the Arab world in the headier days of Arab Nationalism.

** A region of Syria which is part of the larger *Jabal Druze*, i.e., Druze Mountain, area that led a famous revolt in the mid-1920s against the French Mandate. See Chapter 2.

during the Jabal Druze revolt and paid for it by the terrible death he suffered in the dank prison cells. Still, the important thing is that the factory was not torn down after the bankruptcy. The large building stayed there but without machines or workers. We used to go and look at it, enter and find it dark but always clean. Then came the second world war. We didn't experience the horrors of World War I,* but we discovered air raids. The French army turned the factory into a military site. A sort of barracks where dozens of French soldiers and others, who I think were Chinese, lived; it was said they came from Indochina: they were short and yellow-skinned and went almost barefoot in rubber shoes that didn't keep the cold out. They were basically orderlies in the service of the French, cooking the food, brewing the coffee. When off-duty, they'd sing their own songs in a language I couldn't understand even though I tried to be on good terms with them.

During the air raids, the soldiers would go out into the fields. And those other short ones, their little feet in the rubber shoes, darted about the hills, scattering among the ears of wheat, talking with the speed of their strange language.

Naturally, Lebanon gained its independence after the war and the French soldiers left and those little short soldiers went off to their own country. And I think I saw them, or people like them, when they showed films about the Vietnam war on TV.

* * *

They came. Five men, jumping out of a military-like vehicle. Carrying automatic rifles. They surround the house. The neighbors come out to watch. One of them

---

* There was famine in Lebanon during World War I owing to the requisitioning of grain for the soldiers by the Ottoman authorities and to hoarding by grain merchants.

smiles, she makes the victory sign. They come up to the house. Knock on the door; my mother opens, surprised. Their leader asks about me. He's out. — Where did he go? — I don't know. — Come in, have a cup of coffee.

They enter. They search for me in the house. I wasn't there. They search the books and the papers. I wasn't there. They find a book with a picture of Abdel-Nasser on the back cover. I wasn't there. They overturn the papers and the furniture. They curse the Palestinians. They rip my bed up. They insult my mother and this corrupt generation. I wasn't there. Their leader stood, an automatic rifle across his shoulder, in his hand a pistol, threatening.

— He'd better not come back here.

I wasn't there. My mother was there. Trembling with distress and resentment, pacing up and down the house angrily. She stopped answering their questions and left them. She sat on a chair in the entrance, guarding her house as they, inside, looked for the Palestinians and Abdel-Nasser and international communism. She sat on a chair in the entrance, guarding her house. And they, inside, tore up papers and memories. She sat on a chair. And they made the sign of the cross, in hatred or in joy.

They went out into the street, their hands held high in gestures of victory. And some people watched and made the victory sign.

* * *

The big cars stream in, filling the streets. Military-like vehicles, painted black, horns blaring as they go by. Men with automatic rifles jump out. One of them looks through the binoculars dangling from his neck, darting from one corner of the street to the other. They shout at people and tremble with hatred. Their leader looks through the binoculars dangling from his neck, stops to answer the questions of passers-by. He tells them about the siege of Qarantina. We'll mop up every last bit of it and throw them out of Lebanon. We'll defeat them and all the beggars trying to plunder our country.

He gets into his military-like Chevrolet and speeds off. The men scuttle in all directions at once. They march down the streets in step. Han-doy, han-doy (a military expression meaning one-two* which the militiamen in our neighborhood used. I don't know why, but it was current practice).

Cars roaming the streets. The cars gnaw at the streets with their teeth. The big cars blast their sirens. I stand in front of them: their tires are huge, high, and thick.

Black metal devouring me: roadblocks, they say. I see my face tumbling to the ground. Black metal devouring me: my voice slips down alone and stretches to where the corpses of my friends lie buried in mass graves. Black metal devouring me: the raised hands do not wave banners, they clutch death. Metal on the street, terror and empty gas-bottles, corpses and smuggled cigarette cartons. The moment of victory has come. The moment of death has come. War has come. And my mother shakes her head and tells me about the poor.

* * *

They call it Little Mountain. And we called it Little Mountain. We'd carry pebbles, draw faces and look for a puddle of water to wash off the sand, or fill with sand, then cry. We'd run through the fields — or something like fields — pick up a tortoise and carry it to where green leaves littered the ground. We made up things we'd say or wouldn't

---

* A corruption of the French "un-deux," obviously meant ironically by the author.

say. They call it Little Mountain, we knew it wasn't a mountain and we called it Little Mountain.

One hill, several hills, I no longer remember and no one remembers anymore. A hill on Beirut's eastern flank which we called mountain because the mountains were far away. We sat on its slopes and stole the sea. The sun rose in the East and we'd come out of the wheatfields from the East. We'd pluck off the ears of wheat, one by one, to amuse ourselves. The poor — or what might have been the poor — skipped through the fields on the hills, like children questioning Nature about Her things. What we called a *'eid* was a day like any other, but it was laced with the smell of the *burghul* and *'araq* that we ate in Nature's world, telling it about our world which subsists in our memory like a dream. Little Mountain was just a tip of rock we'd steal into, wonderous and proud. We'd spin yarns about our miseries awaiting the moments of joy or death, dallying with our feelings to break the monotony of the days.

They call it Little Mountain. It stretched across the vast fields dotted with prickly-pear bushes. The palm tree in front of our house was bent under the weight of its own trunk. We were afraid it would brush the ground, crash down to it, so we suggested tying it with silken rope to the window of our house. But the house itself, with its thick sandstone and wooden ceilings, was caving in and we got frightened the palm tree would bring the house down with it. So we let it lean farther day by day. And every day I'd embrace its fissured trunk and draw pictures of my face on it.

We feared for the mountain and for its plants. It edged to the brink of Beirut, sinking into it. And the prickly-pear bushes that scratched our legs were dying and the palm tree leaning and the mountain edging toward the brink.

They call it Little Mountain. We knew it wasn't a mountain and we called it Little Mountain.

* * *

When I was three, the parish priest came in his long black cassock and handsome beard. He sat in our house and we all gathered around him in a circle. He started telling us anecdotes and stories. Then, he told us about the achievements of Stalin and the Bolsheviks. He turned to me, ruffled my hair, and told my mother that it was time I was dedicated to Saint Anthony and was given his habit to wear (wearing St. Anthony's habit is a tradition among most of the Eastern Christians in our country; it is worn by children in blessed remembrance of the first Christian monk to have left the city and gone to Sinai to start up the church's first monastic order).

The habit is brown with a white cord dangling from the waist. I walk down the street imitating the gestures of saints. I walk and around me are children who wear or don't wear the habit. We proceed in a long line to where the golden icons lie and the glass is tinted by the sun. And when I forget that I have become a saint, I run wild, playing in the gravel and the sand. I fall down in the streets. Then, when I go home, my mother looks over the saint's soiled habit and slaps and scolds me. Then orders me to kneel down and pray. I kneel down and pray so that the saints might forget that I abandoned them and went off to play with the other children.

I walk, proud in my beautiful brown habit, imitating the priest's gestures. I go to school, vaunting my clothes and put a round halo of leaves on my head.

The parish priest died all of a sudden. I didn't understand what it meant. I remember crying because my sister wept. Then, about six months later as I recall (maybe I no longer actually remember the event but have it imprinted in my memory because of the dozens of times my mother told me the story), I went to church with my mother and father. It was the custom to take off the monk's beautiful garment in church, where it was placed at the altar and candles were lit in offering.

We went to church. I was feeling joyful and rapturous. We reached the heavy door that was always open. It was shut. My father knocked on the door, no one opened. My mother knocked, no one opened. My father said what shall we do. I knocked on the door, kicked it. Leave the habit at the door, answered my mother.

— And the candles?

— We'll light them next week.

I knocked on the door, kicked it. No one opened. My father helped me out of the habit. I began to cry. My mother took the habit, placed it at the door and made the sign of the cross. I was in tears. My father held me by the hand and we walked home. No one opened the church door. We left the habit at the door, and I went home miserable. No candles were lit the following week.

* * *

They came.

Five men, jumping out of a military-like jeep, carrying automatic rifles. Five men wearing big black hats with big black crosses dangling from their necks. They surround the house. They ring the church bells and bang on the door.

Five long black crosses dangling before my mother as she opens the door. She mutters unintelligible phrases. She slams the door shut in their faces and cries.

Five men break down the door and ask for me. I

wasn't there. They find a book with a picture of Abdel-Nasser on the back cover. I wasn't there. My mother was there, trembling with distress, resentment, and fear. My mother was there. She sat on a chair in the entrance, guarding her house as they, inside, looked for the Palestinians and Abdel-Nasser and international communism. She sat on a chair in the entrance, guarding her house as they, inside, tore up papers and memories.

My mother was there.

I wasn't there.

I was in the East, searching with short, almost barefoot men in rubber shoes that didn't keep the cold out. I was in the East, looking for Little Mountain stretched across the frames of men, the sea surging out of their beautiful eyes.

Chapter 2

The
CHURCH

SCENE ONE

Nine p.m. Drizzle and the sound of gunfire getting closer
with every step. We run cautiously, clutching rifles and
dreams. We leap across a very long street, called France
Street, to take up a new position at the end of it: the church.
The voice of the unit commander is resolute and clipped.
Go in carefully. Don't shoot unless absolutely necessary and
only at a visible enemy. According to our reconnaissance
information, they've abandoned the church and set up their
fortified positions on Hwoyek Street. We race down the
middle of France Street. We can see the church ahead
but we can't see anything in the dense darkness, broken
only by flashes of the Doushka* up there close to the sky
where the Murr Tower silences the Holiday Inn keep-
ing Wadi Abu Jameel** out of range of the isolation-

---

    * Heavy machine-gun of Eastern European origin, usually mounted on
a tripod on the back of a pick-up truck. Like Kalashnikov, it has become a generic
name for anything of that description in the military parlance of Lebanon's war.
    ** The Murr Tower is an unfinished concrete high-rise, adjacent to Bei-
rut's Hotel Sector over which a famous battle was fought in 1976. The tower was
then, and has been ever since, a strategic vantage-point, commanding the whole
of Beirut, for the succession of militias that have been able to capture it. The Holiday Inn Hotel was the site of fierce fighting in the battle for the whole sector.
Wadi Abu Jameel is an area of mainly narrow streets just off the Hotel Sector.

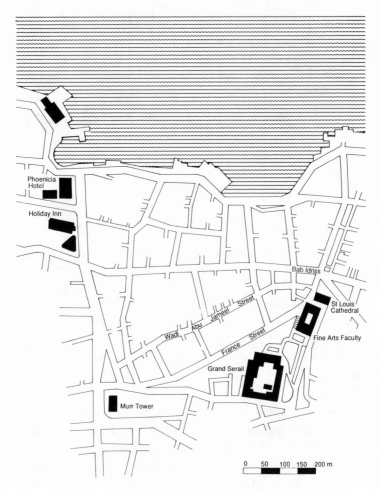

Phoenicia
Hotel

Holiday Inn

Bab Idriss

St Louis
Cathedral

Wadi Abu Jameel Street

France Street

Fine Arts Faculty

Grand Serail

Murr Tower

0 50 100 150 200 m

BAB IDRISS QUARTER

ists'* gun-fire. If they want a battle, they'll have to fight in the streets, for the tall safe building is no longer of any use. We rule the streets, Sameer says. I run, the thin rain trickling between my hand and the rifle butt. The church—I see it, don't see it. Our dreams are right there in the street, and the shells fly and crash into the small, low buildings. 'Atef greets us. Fighting comrades from the various organizations and parties deploy themselves in the buildings and amid the fallen stone. And the sounds of the battle grow louder.

The unit commander is up in front, leading us toward the east. The church is in the east.

We come up from behind. Through the torn-down electricity cables, puddles of water, and mounds of sand. Going through the fine-arts school, we can see the fire the *fedayeen* have lit in front of their bedding, on the platform that was once a stage. We come up from behind and race down a broad street, bullets exploding in the air and on the pavement.

—Deploy.

We deploy.

The first group jumps through the window. Five minutes of silence when every breath is held and fingers stiffen around triggers. The second group jumps. Darkness. We scatter. Then everyone moves forward. The unit commander assigns the groups to their places. We block off all approaches. Darkness, gunfire, not a soul.

Guard-duty is assigned, hide-outs secured.

Butros is walking around looking for the church.

—Butros, we're *in* the church.

—But I don't see anything. Butros takes a taper and lights it in a corner of the church. A pale light quivers. Salem stands up, with his short hair and tall stature; he's like

* A term used by leftists, Palestinians, and nationalists to designate the Phalangists.

the carpet-seller I saw as a child carrying the streets on his shoulders. Salem carries the B-7 rocket launcher on his shoulder, and laughs that soft laugh which rings out between the walls. What's this? This isn't a church.

Christ is on the floor. The statue of Christ lies twisted on the ground, his right cheek to the floor, his left hand open toward the sky, searching for his broken right hand. The picture of the Virgin practically smashed. Water everywhere. The rain coming in through the windows. Christ stretches his left hand out near the window to catch the rain but it trickles between his fingers and nothing remains in his hand save a wetness that recalls the rain.

—What's this? cries Salem. This is a smashed up church.

—Quiet!

Sameer improvising on the Grinov* and shells of all kinds raining down on us. The first battle in the church. We plunge ahead like arrows, in a blast of noise, then everything is quiet. Our groups slip through, striking deep. Sameer on the Grinov and Jaber firing like someone embracing the rain. The sacrament is complete. We've got to know the church—every stone, every recess, every smashed figure—as we pounce, advance, and conquer. We've silenced them. The church is a support position, the commander says. Tomorrow, we'll go on to new positions and take the Bab Idriss intersection. We've no losses—except for Ahmed's slight wound. Rest now and be careful.

Butros in the corner lights his taper and hums faint tunes to himself. I move up and sit beside him. A pale light flutters with the movement of the wind and shapes stretch across the long empty space, empty but for the broken benches, strewn vessels, and twisted statues. Butros gets up and begins to look around. He takes Christ's hand, stands him upright. Christ stands up with his one outstretched

---

* Another machine-gun of Eastern European origin.

hand. Butros sets off, I fall into step. He picks up a priest's brown robe lying in a dark corner. Look. He shouts. We look. Things tremble against the wall and spaces lengthen.

He stands at the altar, in his right hand the B-7 rocket launcher transformed into a priest's staff. Softly intoning a Latin chant,* his voice rises gradually. All eyes turn to the priest standing in his brown robe with his staff and his beard tracing endless circles to the chant. The voice soars. The melody pierces the walls, the words as pebbles under our feet. Eyes widen and the priest grows tall against the wall, advances gradually, swaying. Between phrases, a few shells and red and green shots.**

—Hey Butros, what's this?

Childhood springs forth: the church at Deir al-Harf, before its walls were clad in Romanian colors and Byzantine icons, when it was naked like the *fedayeen*. Father Morkos, hands crucified, voice subdued, rising toward the entrance of the sanctuary where stands a boy, rapt with joy. Latin supplications, Byzantine chants, the priest in our eyes. The window is lit up in the colors of the tracer bullets. Butros carries on.

—Don't you hear? says Salem.

—What?

—I hear footsteps, up there. Be careful.

Butros carries on, three of them cluster together. Altar attendants, in their jackets, standing there riveted, marveling at the game.

—Don't you hear?

The sound of footsteps grows louder. Butros falls silent. Then, suddenly, he wrenches off his priestly robe, clutches his weapon tight. We scatter. The unit commander jumps to his feet, advances. He goes up the stairs,

---

* That is a Roman Catholic chant, not one in the Latin language.

** These refer to the so-called tracer bullets which give off colored (usually red and green) sparks in the night sky and are often used in Lebanon for shooting on joyful occasions like a feast or a wedding, sometimes even a ceasefire.

with three comrades behind him. Caution. A battle inside the church? It would have to be an unusual battle.

The four of them return. Nothing. The church's two priests are still here, and he points upstairs. At first, they thought we were Kataeb,* then when they discovered who we were they got very frightened. I reassured them. I asked them not to light a fire and to stay inside the church at least until morning.

Sounds of nearby shelling and of gunfire getting closer. Christ falls to the ground again. Butros stands him up, but he falls once more.

—Impossible, the base is broken.

—But he'll stand up.

—Even if he stands now, he'll fall tomorrow. The battle's tomorrow, Butros.

SCENE TWO

—What's the difference between war and civil war?

In the interstices between one shot and the next, Salem would find the time to ask such questions. He'd ask the question and not wait for the answer. He'd always say it's not the answer that's important. All answers are the same. The thing is to ask the questions. Between questions, muscles would color and faces lift from the sand and rubble, looking for the narrow streets leading to the sea.

The sea's our goal, the commander says. Once we control the Bab Idriss intersection, we open up the sea road ahead of us. Rabee', the sailor-turned-fighter, knows the taste of the sea and the sea road. That's why he flexes like an arrow.

—I'm a master of answers.

Yet Salem goes on asking: What's the difference between war and civil war?

The narrow streets twist and curve, on either side

---

* The Arabic term for Phalangists.

rock smashed against rock. The sound of the shells crashing against our bodies. To the right, fires, to the left, a low building sagging like an old woman, her joints broken by the shells. Between our line of vision and the sea are build-ings and walls and metal. Between the shell and the scream, stone falls against stone.

The narrow street stretches endlessly. Between its beginning and the positions, sounds of footfalls, of groups of fighters shouting and laughing. The narrow street con-tracts. There is rubble where there should be mounds of sand and sand between the streets and the buildings. Be-tween the hand that fires and the foot that jumps, a body crouches, straightens, crawls. When it arrives, it'll be hold-ing nothing but the sea.

—What does the war want?

—The war doesn't want anything. But it's saying that the asphalt extends the street to the street opposite. And that on the opposite street there are enough metal studs* to make a graveyard.

—Reinforced concrete is resistant. But thick sand-stone gives you more of a sense of security. The streets criss-cross. But gunfire can open holes in the net, and the fish escape to occupy the sea.

It was four in the morning when we began. The sound of the fighting was growing louder and closer after a two-hour lull. Nabeel was holding his gear tight. The walls beginning to be pierced: first the explosive charge against the wall, then the hands and the hammers coming to widen the breach. Moving from hole to hole, clouded in dust, rubble, and noise. Between each hole, bodies stooped, and we advanced. The fighting was growing louder, drowning our voices and the racket from our breaking through the walls. Walls were the new measure of distance. Our blue

---

* A reference to the large, round studs across a street which formerly were used to designate a pedestrian crossing, what in French is known as a *pas-sage clouté*.

jackets were turning white and our hands were covered with the damp dust blowing off the walls. With every wall, we were saving ourselves a street and advanced.

—This is the real Beirut. Talal was saying, covered in dust from head to toe, and laughing with a ring of pride. We've learned war and invented new laws.

—We haven't invented anything yet, said Rabee'. We'll invent when we get to the sea.

As for Nabeel, he was busy opening up new holes, his body bent over the explosive.

Everyone plugged his ears. The commander was moving back and forth between the passageways of the war and those of the church, making sure of the support groups' progress. Voices rose and bodies slipped through the dust.

—When will we get there?

Talal was smiling as he told me the story of Monte Cristo. They wrote a novel about him because of one hole he opened in a prison wall. How many novels will be written about us then who've opened twenty holes in twenty walls? Down with literature, Nabeel shouted. Careful now. This is the last hole. And then we're there and we take them by surprise. Features were hued a bronze-red despite the dust. Everyone looked at his weapon, entrusting it with his last secrets, renewing his pledge of trust in it once again.

Between the last dust and the dust from the shells, the moments were fleeting and shots encircled the air. We ran. Reached the first position, advanced. A wave of dust and voices washing over us as we grasped the pavement and broke it. A few moments of *allahu akbar** mingling with the rustle of clothes against bodies. And then, everything was still. We were at the Bab Idriss intersection. Khaled was killed and three comrades wounded. It wasn't grief so much as something else. When we gathered the following day to

---

* That is, God is great, the Muslim incantation uttered at every call to prayer and often used to express surprise, admiration, or encouragement; it is also used in battle charges as a rallying cry.

assess the battle, Jaber said: an excellent battle. I don't remember much, but I kept shooting till the rifle ran dry. We were like lightning. As for Talal, he was still in a daze. It's like a film, like the movies. Next time, I'll film it.

We were scattered across the buildings and the pavements. Feet soaked, bodies slippery, the drizzle coming and going. We'd carried the sandbags over from the ambush opposite which the Kataeb had abandoned. We'd built our barricades and sat down to eat. We were hungry but ate without appetite.

The surprise came in the afternoon. The positions were quiet and we heard only distant gunfire. Rifles at rest and we resting beside them, on our guard, looking into the distance where the enemy positions were. We were going over our memories of the battle, some true, some not, when we saw throngs of people approaching. Children with heads shaven and unshaven. Milling about the hide-outs, searchings for things in the rubble and in the shops. People of all sorts: Kurds, Arabs. . . . They were all there, with their women and their children.

—Impossible, I shout. We're against looting. We're here to protect the people, not to loot.

—What's impossible is to stop them, Talal retorts, yelling at them to go away, firing a few shots in the air.

But they won't go away. What's this? What is this? Shapes and colors of all sorts bending over. This isn't looting. This is folklore. This is a *'eid*. This is Revolution. All revolutions are like this. Beautiful and terrifying and . . .

In the throes of our surprise and amid everyone's shouting to try to stop them, their numbers grew. They scuttled away from our shouting and firing only to come back. Then khaki began to mingle with the other colors. What's this comrades? Whole groups of them were streaming in. They'd found out that the position had fallen. And had come to fight and loot and live.

—What do they want?

—That's the sea for you. What's the difference between people and the sea? What's the difference between the sea and the fish?

The sea wasn't the only surprise. As it spreads, war gets to be full of surprises. And after the fall of Maslakh and Qarantina* to the Fascists, the war itself became one big surprise. Vast numbers of fighters and militiamen, with their weapons, their boots, their clothes, filling the streets of Wadi Abu Jameel in ceaseless attempts to reach the sea. Practically speaking, coordination wasn't possible. Joint and disjointed forces** from all over the country coming here to fight. The commander going from position to position, trying to coordinate—not an easy task. And we, fighting from position to position, from wall to wall, dust filling the air.

Butros comes running from the church. Panting, he tells us: some of the pews have been taken. A whole lot of them came and covered the walls with their slogans. The two priests are very upset (by the way I forgot to mention that the two priests stayed in the church and struck up a firm friendship with Talal).

—What shall we do?

—Nothing. Protect the church and the two monks. Then there were shouts and explosions every-

---

* Maslakh, abattoir in Arabic, was an area adjacent and similar to Qarantina (see note, p. 10) and also the site of the government-controlled slaughterhouse. The two areas were fiercely bombed and finally razed to the ground during late 1975 through January 1976 in notorious atrocities that culminated in scenes of hysterical rejoicing by Phalangist militiamen uncorking bottles of champagne amid corpses heaped on the ground.

** The joint forces (al-quwwāt al-mushtaraka) refer to the loose coalition of anti-Phalangist Lebanese organizations and parties (ranging from the Communists to Islamic groupings) allied with and fighting alongside the PLO in the period 1975–1982.

where. Fighters shooting and looting. Competing with the children for the small items. A new group arrived, fighting savagely in the middle of the street. Looking for war, amid the cries and the cold.

Seeing them darting about in the middle of the street, screaming, I didn't understand. I watched them. Rage trickled through their fingers and their teeth. They got to the music shop and broke down the door. Seizing trumpets, drums and cymbals, the musical procession set off down the middle of France Street, full of percussion, shouting, and gunfire. Another martyr. The streets made way for them and the war opened its doors to their tears.

I reached the church and went on watching them from the window. Butros was sitting in a corner all by himself, humming his Latin melody. I sat down beside him and heard the footsteps of the two priests upstairs going up to the window and watching.

My voice began to rise, Butros beside me correcting the rhythm of the funerary chant I sang.

SCENE THREE

The two Capuchins are still here. Father Marcel, about 80, and his companion whose name I couldn't remember and whose age I couldn't tell, for old age seeped through his fingers like water. They stayed in their room above the church, not mixing with the comrades. I knew that they viewed us with extreme suspicion and alarm. We doubted their motives for staying and they feared us and our intentions. That's why I was surprised when the commander asked me to go out and buy them some food — milk, cheese, canned things, meat, coffee. . . . I went, bought the stuff, and on my way back got hold of a bottle of French wine through a friend. I told myself we'd celebrate with the two priests. They were delighted with the present but objected to the cheese.

—We want French cheese.

—That's not possible, Father. All the shops are closed or ransacked. I nevertheless went and bought them some vile French cheese which used to be sold every-where—that same cheese my mother would force me to eat though I could never see that it had any taste. We went up to their room, Butros, Talal and I. They were eating.

—Why don't you taste the wine?

—I'm waiting for you, Father Marcel answered me. We're going to celebrate together with this wine. We went back down the stairs. Father Marcel was aghast; he trem-bled with dismay and grief.

—What's all this? What is it? This is a barbaric war.

—All wars are like this, Father. It's nothing.

—No, no. Not all wars are like this. I've been in a war too. I was an officer in the French army during the First World War. That war wasn't like this. We respected places of worship and we didn't harm civilians.

—But this is a civil war. It's the civilians who're fighting.

We were walking side by side. Father Marcel bend-ing down silently, fearfully, over the statues strewn on the ground. Picking up bits of debris, muttering words I couldn't make out, prayers, or curses, or a mixture of both. Look, Father Marcel said. The church is a ship. Look at the architecture: a church is built like a ship. The church is a ship floating above the world. It is in the world but not of it. I'm not sad. This is a barbaric war, and the winds are blowing against our ship and it has been wrecked. But we'll rebuild it.

—I'm afraid the ship might sink, Father, Butros said maliciously.

—No, no. The ship can't sink in the world. It is in it and not of it. It might be wrecked, that's possible. But it can't sink.

I turned to Father Marcel and saw his face extend across the surface of his white hair as he beheld the ship-wreck and its sorrows. This is a man full of memories. These last few moments of his have become memories. Poor Father Marcel.

—But Father, this religious concept about the church, it is common both to you and to the Eastern Christians?

—Naturally, my son. It's an old concept. It was established long before the schisms and the religious wars. The church is a ship and the world a rough sea. No two people disagree over that.

—Then, what *is* the difference? Talal asked.

—That's a very complicated story. But I can tell you that, in principle, the difference has to do with the fundamental view of the relationship between religion and life. *We* are practical, rational people. For us, religion regulates the relationship between God and life, it is rational and organized, it orders things. But Eastern Christians, now they're mystics. In the past, they didn't understand the relationship between religion and the state and now they've become a cover for Communism and atheism.

Father Marcel resumed his tour. He was bowed with grief. His face blended with the church's empty space, empty but for the debris and the remnants of the altar. As he walked, the sound of his footsteps striking the floor grew louder, and straw and the bits and pieces of shells flew about the bottom of his brown robe. The thin sun, tinted by the church's stained glass, reflected its colors on the undulating robe.

Let's go up now, Father Marcel said. Let's drink to my friendship for the *fedayeen*.

Father Marcel opened the bottle of wine like a professional soldier. He filled the glasses and drank to our new friendship. He was happy as a child with the wine but he drank like a soldier.

—Why did you do this to the church? This is no ordinary church. It's a cathedral. Do you know what a cathedral is?

I shrugged my shoulders.

—A cathedral is the central church. The big church. Everyone's church. And yet you went and destroyed it.

—As you can see, Father, we're not the only ones here. There are lots of fighters. Aside from that, the church was almost destroyed when we entered it. And you know that we had to take it: it's a strategic location, and besides the enemy used it to fire on us.

We sat and drank around a small table spread with the cheese and the wine. The other priest sat next to us, eating and drinking, taking no notice of us. I think he was looking at us from under his half-shut eyes with hatred and resentment.

Father Marcel began telling us his story: I came to Lebanon, he said, after World War I. I was a lieutenant in the French army. Then I got to know this country and fell in love with it. I loved two things about it: the commerce and the openness to the West. This is an amazing country, and its people are amazing. I wanted to stay so I did. As to how I became a priest, that's an interesting story. I believed, like all French soldiers, that we were the bearers of a civilizing mission to the oppressed peoples of the Orient. We came here full of dreams. We were coming to the exotic East. To the land of Lamartine, which we were going to rescue from serfdom. Then, after the battles the French army was forced to fight in these lands, I found that the only way to people's hearts was not by the sword but through culture. If they studied in our schools, they'd learn our language, would strengthen their economic ties with us and learn about civilization. At first, I wanted to be a teacher in one of the Catholic schools. The teaching led me to God. You see, I came to religion by way of civilization and not, as is usual with you, civilization being introduced to your countries by way of religion.

Talal blew the smoke from his cigarette into the air, his big eyes looking skeptically at the priest. But Father, you didn't introduce civilization into our countries. You're just colonizers, coming in with the ten commandments. Giving us the commandments and taking the land.

—That's not true. That's the way Communists talk. No, my son, we didn't take anything. We lost our best men to the cause of our civilizing mission. Then we left of our own good will.

—I don't believe you left of your own good will. You left because you were forced to.

Father Marcel wearies of the ideological discussion. He doesn't like ideology. Ideology is the instrument of the age of materialism to ensnare young people. It inevitably leads to people's enslavement to materialism. So they become fanatical and closed to discussion.

—You were a lieutenant in the French army when it entered our country, Father. So you must have taken part in the battle of Maysaloun.*

—Maysaloun, no, I didn't take part in it. I took part in many other battles. In the battles for the Jabal Druze and Ghawtah, outside Damascus. And I recall that we were models of chivalry and discipline, and harmed no one.

---

* It was as a result of the battle of Maysaloun in July 1920 that the French army defeated King Faisal's Arab forces and was able to occupy Damascus and impose France's mandate over Syria.

—But Father, the massacres and excesses of the battles of Ghawtah and the Jabal are well known. I've read General Andrea's book about these battles. He writes with delight about the occupation, and the expulsion of the Druze, and the killing of the rebel groups in Ghawtah.

—General Andrea? He was my friend. Poor General Andrea, he was earnest and romantic, his entire ambition was to become a marshall in the French army, but he died of a heart attack. Poor Andrea. Listen carefully. (Here, the priest's tone sharpened.) War is war. You can't fight your enemies, you can't stop terrorists and spies and the enemies of civilization without killing some of them. The fate of civilization was at stake. The fate of French history hung on the outcome of the Jabal and Ghawtah battles. Leniency was out of the question. Things had to be quick and sharp.

—What's the difference between a priest and a cop, Father Andrea? He'd be wearing a French officer's uniform, holding a gun in his right hand and a glass of wine in the other. He'd tell revolting jokes about the Arab dead who were left out in the open in their black clothes with no one to bury them. . . . We're tough, the officer would say, surrounded by Senegalese and Circassian soldiers who spoke pidgin French and talked about heroism and civilization and women.

—What's the difference between a priest and a cop, Father?

The church was a ship, but the helm was smashed. The church wouldn't sink. And, upstairs, lived two aged priests with their memories and sorrows.

—Why are those who love Western civilization being defeated?

But *we* were looking for the sea.

The church has become a support position. Grinov shots reverberating in the air, Jaber's machine-gun lying silent then bursting forth. Rubble all around. And with us, Father Marcel, his companion and memories of France.

—How will you say mass, Father!

—It'll be a silent mass, he answers me. Amid such cacophony, we seek out silence. We want silence to reign once again. Silence alone is the key to contemplation.

Sameer was talking and telling jokes non-stop, Butros humming his tune, and Talal thinking about his new film. The guns wouldn't hush.

SCENE FOUR

Between the wrecked church and Bab Idriss Square, where the forward positions were, moments blended into one another. The church had become a secondary position, but we stayed in it and it was now our favorite sleeping-place. A large courtyard, thick walls. Coldness and memories. And during the long days, we'd sit between its walls, or around the windows, asking questions and answering them.

—But why didn't you kill me? Father Marcel would say.

—No, Father! Why should we kill you? We may or may not agree with you. But we wouldn't kill you.

—But war is full of killing.

—No, Father. The war is one thing and killing you is another.

Death, here, was an interval. Just an instant of love, or an instant of hatred. A moment to step into, a moment to wait for. Talal was always talking to me about death. What is death? You feel nothing. Just like that, all of a sudden, you feel nothing. You open the door, then you step in, then nothing. I'd look at his eyes and see them widening. What's the relationship between death and wide-open eyes?

The battles were a lesson. But death—that's something else. I carried him across my shoulder, he quivered like a bird.

Death is a bird, Butros would say.

But we fight to win, not to die, Jaber would shout.

We die for the sake of a poster, I answered. The color photograph, with the colored writing underneath, and the tear-filled eyes of the young girls behind.

—No way, Father. We wouldn't kill you.

And the prisoner, what shall we do with the prisoner? Ahmed would ask.

—Kill him on the spot. This is a war without prisoners. They kill you without justification. They kill you because your name is what it is and not something else.* They skin our dead and finish off the wounded. This is a war without prisoners. Prisoners are killed on the spot.

The bird on my shoulder was quivering. My face wet with hot blood, and his body stretching from my hand to the world's end. The bird making his last lament, the sea and the rain all around him. I darted between the shells and the explosions. Then I put him down beside me. I sat and talked to him. A child, his face fondled by the breeze, a child who wouldn't cry. I carried him again. When I reached the hospital, the doctor told me he was dead. I didn't understand a thing. I returned to my companions and we went on shooting and advancing, and laughed and told jokes.

—No, we wouldn't kill the prisoner, but take him and put him inside Father Marcel's brown robes. Butros leaped to his habit, put it on, and raised his hand bidding

---

* A reference to sectarian killings, one's religion very often being evident from one's name. For an Arab, Ahmed would obviously be a Muslim and Butros (Peter in English) a Christian.

us be silent, humming his Latin chant. We left him alone with his rituals and dreams.

I was walking about the hall of St. Louis Cathedral. This is an old church, a very old church. Maybe it was built in the age of the church missions. Maybe it was built by the first silk merchant to arrive in Beirut from Lyons, in fulfillment of a vow he made for the success of his commerce. The fact is that I forgot to ask the priest about the history of the church, how it was built and since when there has been a community called the Latins in our country. The important thing is the organ. Lying on the floor, broken, moaning, its beautiful melodious sound gone. And everywhere, the remnants of smashed floor tiles and water from the rain. The thick walls white but pock-marked, with multi-colored graffiti, black and red and green, all over. And between a holy statue and an ancient icon, you can read: *allahu akbar*, Fateh* was here. And all around, the sounds of percussion and the echo. I didn't used to understand what an echo was. When we were little, we would go to the *wadi* overlooking Nahr Beirut and shout, and our voices returned, repeated over and over again. But here the echo has a different beat. One shell becomes a whole battle. The echo mingles with the sound of glass and the rattle of the censer and the pacing of the priests' footsteps.

—The ship's been wrecked, Father.

The church had turned into something like an abandoned house. Blankets on the floor, empty bullet cases, the rhythms of our footsteps. In the middle, where the helm and the altar stood, sandbags were being taken to the buildings nearby and echo reigned sovereign over the church.

War destroys everything. But what shall we do with victory?

—We'll take it to the Jordan River. Imagine victory.

---

* The largest organization within the PLO.

Victory means that the poor become the masters and the former masters remain masters but without serfs. The organ will play an eastern mode and our fingerprints will be the flag. We'll take Victory to the Jordan River and John's head will come on a golden platter and they will speak to each other. Then they will go down to the Jordan River together. John will baptize Victory and Victory will carry John's head before it.

—True, if we're victorious here in Lebanon, what will happen?

—Israel will come, and after we defeat her, America will come.

—And after we defeat America, who will come?

—When we defeat America, everyone will go. We will have written the story of the longest and most beautiful war.

—But what?

Talal doesn't agree. Winning isn't important. What's important is something else. What's important is that we live life as it is, take it as it comes, fight, and die on the mountain top.

The church shook with every shell. The body of Christ was still bent over the ground. And the long censer still awaiting the hand that would hold it, but the hand wouldn't come. Everything smashed: brass vessels, small silver spoons, silken robes littering the ground. And then, Jihad discovered the treasure. Innumerable candles. Thin, shiny tapers, in special drawers. He took them and threw them up in the air. We ran, gathering them up. This is a fortune. In the evening, we lit up the entire fortune. One hundred tapers, which we stood on the ground, shining into the night. Between the beat of the censer and the beat of the rain. They cast a brilliant glow such as we'd never known. In it, our bodies seemed slight, our movements shadowless. A hundred tapers flickering in the middle of a ruined church. We're in a real ship. The ship shimmering in the middle of the sea and inside it strange seamen looking for their new clothes. In the middle of the sea, the drizzle falling on the church's red tile roof and running off its sides, all around us waves and priests and pirates' bullets.

Father Marcel comes running and smiles when he sees the candles.

—I thought the church was on fire. No problem, do as you please.

—Thank you, Father.

A tribe around the tribal fire. The lights were dancing but we didn't dance around the fire. We were blowing cigarette smoke into the vast emptiness and looking for the sea.

—What do you think, Father? Why doesn't the ship sink?

Father Marcel doesn't answer, sets off for his memories, telling us stories about the saints, then goes back to asking: Why don't you kill me?

—And why should we kill you, Father? We are together, living close to the sea in a wrecked ship. When we reach the sea, the ship will sink and our story will be over.

The sea's our goal, the commander says, and we are waiting for the sea. We will get there, cast our nets, take off our clothes, and breathe in the smell of the fish. Jihad sits down close to the fire and starts singing. Our voices rise. And from the chorus soars Ahmed's voice, taut, moaning as he traces the future on the broken wall in front of him.

SCENE FIVE

The sea in our eyes. Between the cordons of fire and the salt of the sea, Jaber fell. He fell like an arrow on the mountain top, so the snow mixed with the sea and the rain with the saltiness from the gunbarrel. The battle for the sea was the most difficult, the roads twisting and turning endlessly. We didn't surprise them, nor were we surprised, except when we reached the sea. The raining shells mixing with the sky's own rain, the wind carrying the rifles as much as we did, the battle flowing from balcony to balcony and from trench to trench. The sea was far away, that's why it surprised me. There was darkness and voices and the movement of feet and the suppleness of bodies and fear for one another. All of them things we'd experienced before. But today we were experiencing surprise. We were running, no longer seeing for the thick darkness: just fire and movement which we shot at, advancing, as across the entire area the others shot and advanced.

The smell of salt and fish sprang to my nostrils. We're there, I shouted. I gripped my clothes, unbelieving. The hours of pain vanished. But I wasn't seeing the sea, or hearing anything save the sound of the waves. I breathed in its smell. The smell of the sea spreading through the pores of my body and penetrating the joints that had soaked up the decay of the swamps and hugged sand and dust while looking for the arc stretching from Mount Sanneen* to the shore. The sea was entering our eyes. Searing them, the smell of salt smothered in fishy things flooded our eyes. We were advancing and the sea was ours.

Talal tore off his clothes and threw himself naked into the waves.

—But we're still in the middle of the battle!
—This is the battle.

He swam like someone making love to a woman. Diving in and coming up. He scooped up the water, throw-

---

* The snow-capped peak of Mount Sanneen, one of the highest along the Lebanon range, is visible from most vantage-points in Beirut for many months of the year; it is a potent symbol of Lebanon and used widely in its "mythology."

ing it to the sky. Embracing the cold and the drizzle and the salt. And when he got out he was shivering like a bird.

— You'll get sick and have to leave the battle.

But Talal didn't get sick and didn't leave the battle. From shipwreck to shipwreck, he carried the battle on his shoulders and when he had safely delivered his trust to the sea, he died on the mountain top.

— Jaber's fallen, said Sameer. He was beside me; he was hit in the head and just keeled over. I carried him and ran to the back. Some comrades took him. And now they've come and told me he's dead.

— Death is a bird, Jaber says. It circles above the water, in search of fish, then drops and the fish eat it.

— Death is a sign, butterflies and horses. Death is us, then Butros falls silent. The sea was bleeding salt into his eyes and he wouldn't cry. He was laid out, his head covered with his red *keffieh*,* his eyes half-shut, his clothes spattered with blood and mud. Jaber, graceful as a spear, fallen between church spire and mountain top. He lay there, covered, surrounded by voices and the Palestinian flag. He knew he was going to die, that's why his laugh welled up with every shot. He'd hold his rifle tight, fire and laugh like children holding their toys.

— We'll drape him in the Palestinian flag.

— This isn't the Palestinian flag. Palestine isn't a country for it to have a flag. Palestine is a condition. Every Arab is a Palestinian. Every poor man who carries a gun is a Palestinian. Palestine is the condition of us all.

Palestine used to be a map, but has become the sea. Some day, I'll make a film about the sea, Talal said. I'll sew the sea into a dress and Jaber will give it to his mother as a present.

He was laid out. Surrounded by voices, in his head

---

* The traditional red-and-white checkered Arab head-dress, now the hallmark of the Palestinian fighter.

a single shot, and his laugh ringing through the courtyard. We brought over an empty coffin, put him inside and set off, with him held aloft the upraised palms, the chanting voices, the unbending rifles. A long wooden coffin, inside it, a boy sleeping, surrendering to the hands carrying him.

Look, Butros pointed. The coffin is like a ship. A long wooden ship floating in the sea. The ship sways on the uplifted hands. In front, on the mast a tall flag. And behind, people and fighters, comrades who have come to bear the ship to sea. Inside, Jaber playing captain for the last time, leading us on his new sea voyage through the empty streets.

The priest stood. We put the ship down in front of the altar, and from the pews there rose a soft moaning like the sound of the sea before the breaking of the storm.

This is a *real* church, whispered Salem.

The priest stood, censer in hand, intoning his Byzantine chant. It was a sunny day, color-tinted lights reflected on his long, black clothes and his shining beard. Jaber, inside his ship, couldn't find the words. The voice of the sole chanter in the Ras Beirut* church rose next to the priest's robe. Standing before the wide-eyed icons, listening to the prayer, watching the priest's gestures as he spoke in raised voice about the meaning of martyrdom.

The church a ship, and Jaber in his ship and we inside the vast ship. Outside, the sound of shooting growing louder and the advancing commotion.

We carried him once more and set off. Our footsteps on the asphalt like the oars of ancient mariners steering their boat to shore. Voices subsiding, the sun shining, the upraised hands carrying the wooden rectangle and the ship swaying.

In front of the gaping hole, we came to a stop. We took the ship and placed it inside the sand and earth.

---

* In Arabic, *ras* means head or cape. Thus, Ras Beirut is the headland of the city that juts out into the sea and the name by which that whole area is known.

—The ship has sunk.

—No, it hasn't sunk.

The ship was going into the earth, coming to rest, amid our shooting, the loud chanting, and the priest's voice intoning the last words: from dust thou art and to dust thou shalt return.

I looked at Salem hiding his grief behind the elongated face and the wan smile. He asked me about the war, how will the war end?

—This war won't end, Sameer answered, for death has begun and war has just begun.

There was the silence, the sea, and the ship; but Father Marcel's ship wouldn't sink, it just got wrecked. And Jaber in his ship swaying like a princess, then falling, descending little by little until the earth was level with the ground again and nothing was left but the writing on the walls, the voices and the gunfire.

—What's the difference between a priest and a cop, Father Andrea?

—Why didn't you kill me? asks Father Marcel.

—What's the difference between war and civil war? says Salem.

Death is a bird, says Jaber. And Talal dreams of a sea long as his lover's hair and, carrying camera and rifle, leaps between the waves.

Chapter 3

The
LAST
OPTION

What is it you were doing
In the ancient gardens
Three hundred years ago.
In two instants, your life will end
The Chinese seer told you,
The Chinese seer
The corner.
The fish breathe through your green eyes
And your body washes away the travails of music
And the pain from the silence of the gilded
    sepulchres.
My heart has been weary ever since I beheld you
Somewhere in Asia,
Where the Chinese seer
Played your death song
And danced,
Before he died.

Mohammad Shbaro

The last option is me, I told her as we walked along the
shoreline, our feet in the sand. She, in her brown skin and
laughing African boy's cropped hair, mocks me: you're a ro-

mantic, she says and then falls silent and lets me talk on and on endlessly. I talk, dangling about inside the words, pick up some pebbles, put them in my mouth and carry on talking. Then, when I grab her, she escapes to the sand, puts some on her head and swings it in the air. Then she shouts: stop. And I stop, for I'm not able to. Every night, I go back home, broken, and decide to keep silent from now on. I must walk alongside the lithe young African boy without opening my mouth. Then, she will fall into the trap of language and talk endlessly, the way all women do. And I will nod my head, smile a little, then pronounce my judgment: you're a romantic. But when I'm with her again, my resolve fails and I remain the only romantic. Her neck rises. I don't understand: a lean face and short-cropped hair mingling with the wind and a neck that extends endlessly. When I try to take hold of the neck and rise up to it, I fall down on the sand. You must understand, she would say. My mother understands, I would say. She's waiting for me when I come back, exhausted. She thinks that I don't talk so she doesn't ask. She just gives me a little food but of course I don't eat. My mother is saddened, I grow sad and the long neck that I climb extends endlessly. I stop asking questions and walk beside her, head to the ground. What are those shoes you're wearing, she says. They're *fedayeen's* shoes, I answer her, then we are silent. Her name is Mariam. Of course, I can't run any farther. I follow her, she runs then bends over. Puts sand on her head, as she always does. Go. Why *fedayeen's* shoes? Her laughter rings out and I sink into my shoes, slithering about inside as if they were small ships on a long shore.

> —I'm a *feda'i*.
> —And why are you a *feda'i?*
> —Because I became one.
> —And why did you become one?

—Because, I don't know. Because I love you.
—You're a romantic.
—I'm a prince.
—You're a dog.
—I'm a hero.
—You're a *feda'i*.
—. . .

She laughed. It rang like a bow. The man grasped his bow and let fly. The arrow glanced. It plunged into the sea and began to sink.

—Why are you beyond the sand?

She said she didn't like answering any of my questions.

—Do you know my father?
—I don't know him.
—Do you like my father?
—How can I like someone I don't know.
—You must like him because he's my father.
—I don't like him, I don't like any fathers.
—But my father died.
—All fathers die.
—But he burned alive.
—All fathers burn alive.

I lifted the camera to my shoulder and stood up. I want to film you. Holding the camera, I traced the lithe young African boy against the wall, then drew a circle. Stand in the circle. She stands in the circle. I rotate her and she rotates. She stretches her arms forward, then bends over, becomes a circle.

—Why do you wear trousers? She laughs. She rotates inside herself then falls into the middle of the circle. She stretches her arms to their utmost and her face quivers slightly. I leave her on the ground and raise her to the ceiling of the room. Sand fills up the ceiling, then the face collapses. I get some straw and put it on her head. You're a chicken, I say. Why is there this war? she asks. I'm holding the camera and giving the orders. I'm the director; one actress, the sea, and the sand.

—And how was your father whom I don't like burned alive?

She gets up, brushes the straw off her head, steps out of the circle. I don't like the circle or the cinema.

—But how did your father burn?

—I want to go home. In any case, I don't read the papers and don't like reading them either.

—Where did your father die?

—I've been in Beirut for a long time. Yesterday, my mother said she wanted us to go to Amman. I don't want to go to Amman. I don't like Amman. Do you like Amman?

Amman was a city when I went there. No, it wasn't a city. It was a cluster of hills. I went, the army was readying itself and we were preparing. That's why I didn't get around the city. I would stand in a dugout beside men with brown foreheads, but I no longer remember their names. The gunfire exploded in the air above our heads. But the clash didn't happen. The objective conditions weren't ripe. That's what they told me. Naturally, I was convinced. When objective conditions come into it, you can't but be convinced. And convincing conditions need to be objective. I walked through the streets of Amman alone. I didn't know anybody. The military training course was over and I should have been getting back to Beirut. Amman didn't mean anything except that it was full of *fedayeen*'s shoes, pictures of martyrs, guns and memories of the homeland, and the 1967 defeat. That's why I don't know Amman. I remember it being white. During the September massacres, even the blood seemed white to me. Of course, I don't like that city. None of my friends like it. It's like nothing at all. Maybe it's like the night. My friends died in Amman but that doesn't change anything.

She dances on the ceiling, then slides to the wall. The first city was a clump of sand, stone, and rubble. The lithe young boy is on the ceiling. He bends, rotates upon himself, breaks in two. He falls from the ceiling to the floor. The camera carries him to my hands. I switch on the electricity. Did you like the film? Next time, I'll carry the sand and the salt within a rhythm I haven't yet discovered. When a woman bends down inside it, the circle grows more beautiful. It becomes like bread or like an orange.
— But you don't know Amman.

— Name.
— Talal. Talal Saleh.
— Occupation.
— Student at the Engineering School.
— Why are you demonstrating?
— All the students are demonstrating and I'm demonstrating like them.

The police, red-faced, carrying white truncheons, white shields, and tear-gas. Weeping, we attack them. Some of them have gas masks and some are crying without their masks. They're shaking. And we run in the middle of the streets, ripping down powerlines and road signs. We attack Beshara al-Khoury's statue,* gird it with metallic wire. The truncheons are white, the shields are white, the cops cry and we cry. The officer: you, and he points to me.

---

* Beshara al-Khoury was the first president of independent Lebanon. His statue, on one of Beirut's main arteries, was a major point of convergence for demonstrators during the worker and student protest era of the late '60s and early '70s.

You're the one responsible for this. My hand sinks into my pocket, my shirt falls out and hangs over my trousers. I don't answer. Scores of policemen are wounded. The officer shouts: you are responsible. I slide to the corner. The king is the one who's responsible. Then I go home, as usual.

"What is it you were doing in the ancient gardens three hundred years ago."

My father knows Amman. And my mother insists on going there. She's scared of the shells. I also hate wars. I know what you're going to say. She put her finger to her lips to silence me. But I hate war, and especially just wars. I love my father. When he went away the last time, he never came back. Even his shoes didn't come back. I asked the officer—he was a friend of my father's—to give me his clothes or his shoes or any other thing. There was nothing left. When we went to the cemetery, he was inside the coffin. And he descended into the earth in the coffin. He burned alive. I didn't understand anything. We never grasp the fundamental things in life, that's why we stop at details. That day, I discovered Amman. It's a cluster of mountains, that's what people always say. But it's a succession of impenetrable circles; broad streets and hollow slogans running through them, but a succession of circles nevertheless; with the blood oozing out all around turning into circular blotches. The city cannot become an orange. The tanks came while we were there. My father wasn't there because he'd died before that. He died in the shelling, when the planes did whatever they pleased. Everybody scattered. My father scattered. He raised his head and the gun in his hand fired shots you couldn't hear because the sound of the planes was the only thing you could hear. Then the shell came. It was the tanks which divided the city into circles.

We survived. The thirst, and my mother cursing them all and my father's picture hanging on the wall.

The lithe young African boy stretches his neck, laughing. Those are old memories. But he died. Death is far off, she said. That's why rituals were created. Crying and wailing and dancing and standing for a long time in front of the grave. Death approaches, hand and bald head. The city we call white fills up with pictures and corpses and posters. Serhan Beshara Serhan's face* leaps out in front of the American revolutionary tourist.

—What's that?

—A poster. We consider Serhan a hero. "I killed for my country."

—But he's a terrorist and an enemy of democracy.

—And I'm a terrorist, I said to the American tourist. But I can hold you and kiss you and laugh. She laughed a white laugh.

The young boy bent over the sand, plunged his hand into a damp spot, and sat. You talk a lot, he'd say. My mother says I don't talk. And wonders to herself why she has lived to know such dark days. Then she tells me the story for the hundredth time, and I listen to it for the hundredth time. She always forgets the madman's story. Be quiet, you're mad. There's no madman's story, you're just an intelligent boy. All those who saw you said, Imm Ahmed you must perfume him with incense and take him to Hajjeh Fatmeh.** I used to perfume you with incense, feed you sugar and almonds, and give you money. But you were a clever child.

---

* Serhan was the young Palestinian who assassinated United States senator Robert Kennedy in 1968.

** Abu Ahmed and Imm Ahmed, literally father and mother of Ahmed; it is common in many parts of the Arab world to refer to people in this way, and even childless or sonless married men and women may be given such a *laqab*—agnomen or nickname—as a sign of respect.

Hajjeh is the feminine of *haajj*, i.e., someone who has accomplished the required Muslim pilgrimage to Mecca. Such people are often credited with

Instead of buying balloons and sweets, you used to go to the shop and buy a little bit of everything, then stand in front of the house and open up a store. And the children of the neighborhood would come and buy from your shop, God be blessed. A half pound would become three pounds. Of course, I contributed to your brisk trade because I'd give my sister's children money to go and buy things from your shop. But you made the profit. I told myself, Imm Ahmed, this boy will become a merchant, he will open shops and build buildings. But look at what you're doing with yourself now. Joining political parties and the *fedayeen*, you're not going to become a merchant.

But my mother won't tell me the madman's story. And I have forgotten it.

I didn't understand and I think Salem, the tall one, doesn't understand it either. Shots and cries and explosions everywhere. The ground catching fire. We run, sit aside panting. He's holding the B-7 rocket-launcher firm on his shoulder. You've got to cover me, he says. I move up and open fire. He shoots his rocket. The blasts, the smell, the flame. Shop doors are smashed, so let everything burn. To-morrow, the women will come along in their long *abayahs** to sort the smell of gunpowder from things and go. The shops must burn down.

The brown African boy bending over. Amman was a

---

baraka, a special sort of blessing, a favorable influence or touch to which children should be exposed if possible, especially if they have experienced some misfortune, illness, or disability. The term is often used to precede a name in deference to a person's age or perceived wisdom even if the pilgrimage has not actually been undertaken.

    * Any of a variety of long flowing robes worn throughout the Middle East by men or women. Although originally used to designate the long, woolen cloaklike wrap worn especially in the desert where the nights are cold, it has become a generic term for any kind of floor-length, loose garment.

succession of white circles. I grab her and throw her to the ceiling. Look. She looks at her body stretching upward.

—Why are you doing this to me?

—Cinema is cinema, I tell her. Life is a deception. Her laugh rings out between her bare ankles. Look at the color of the sea, she says. The sea isn't blue, the sky isn't blue. That is the real deception, you see.

—I see that the sky's blue and the sea's blue. That's what I see, I told her.

—Can you see green? Can you see light blue? Of course, you can't see white. You're sand. We all walk on the sand, then we become sand. I want to plunge in there between the green and the purple. In the dividing instant. There I want to build a house or a tent or a clump of stones, or drown. That's what drowning is. Total surrender. It is objects which bend. Have you seen objects when they bend? But I can't. Nobody can. No one can separate colors, we can only mix them. And when colors start to intermingle, they never stop. Even blending is impossible. Colors have their own temperaments and histories. One color goes into another, then becomes a hint of something and enters into objects; colors dissolve in colors. White doesn't exist, she said. The young African boy took an apple, bit into it, put it on his head and began to run. The apple fell. Where's the apple, she said. The apple mixes with the sand and the sand blends into the water. Mud. That's straw, she said. The color of the apple changes. But it's still on my head. It's on the ground, I told her, and bent down to pick it up. Leave it, she screamed. The apple's on my head. You don't see anything, she said. No one sees. But it's on my head. And I have to travel tomorrow. I can't leave my mother on her own. Could you leave your mother?

—I don't know, but I always leave her.

—I never leave my mother. She wants to go to Amman, I'll go with her.

—And me?

—You! What do you want from me?

—We'll get married, like everybody else.

The lithe young African boy laughed. I'm not going to get married. And if I do get married, it won't be to you. I'm not going to marry a man who's going to die.

—All men die.

—But you're a *feda'i*. I like the *fedayeen* but I would never marry one because they die quickly.

—All *fedayeen* get married.

Colors nearing. Talal sat alone on the sand. He took off his glasses, wiped them carefully, and put them back on. The shore welcomed the gentle waves and sent them off again. In the damp place on the edge of the sea the circles multiplied. That's the difference. He went up to the shore. These are colors. Colors only take on their color the moment they sink. The sea unraveled into endless circles. He took some sand and threw it to the sea. Everything sinks in water. Talal bent down. Where are you, lithe young African boy?

"What is it you were doing in the ancient gardens three hundred years ago."

My voice drowned in the first circle, to my left. I took off my shoes, held them in my hand, and walked off. I got into the car. Turned on the engine. It crackled, then moaned and spluttered before the car would move forward. Where are you, lithe young African boy? I stopped the car in front of the bakery. Bought a hot loaf and began chewing slowly, the trees planted on either side of the street curling around the electricity poles. And I breathed in the smell of the bread.

* * *

Everything's ready, says Nabeel. But we're late and the boys are waiting. Talal looks at his watch, we must go immediately. Nabeel is jumping up and down. What are you doing? I ask him.

—I'm getting ready.

—But we're not going to a football match.

—That's how I get ready, says Nabeel.

—What's the news from Maslakh and Qarantina? asks Salem.

—No news yet, but the position's extremely difficult.

—I don't like this food. Bread and *zaatar!** It's not food for fighters, says Talal.

The commander speaking: it's breakfast. And we've got to eat it quickly. Nabeel laughs like a real teacher.

—Don't laugh teach, I don't like bread and *zaatar*.

—Look at what you do to yourself Talal. Why do you complicate things, boy? It's all dough. Here we put the *zaatar* inside the bread, there they put it inside the *kaaka*.**

—I want to buy a *kaaka*.

It isn't a question of price, really Abu Ahmed. A *kaaka* costs 10 piastres, may God ruin no one. But the kid must learn to obey. My mother talks on and on. I look at my father. The slight, wizened man in ragtag clothes winks at me.

---

* Thyme. In Lebanon, Syria, and Palestine, it is dried and crushed then mixed with other herbs and spices, such as sumac, sesame seed, salt, and cumin, and is eaten in a paste made from adding olive oil to the mixture. It is widely used as a breakfast or dinner condiment with bread and tea.

** *Kaak*, singular *kaaka*, is a generic term used for a variety of slightly sweet or savory, always dry, baked goods in the shape of a bracelet, similar to pretzels.

—Walk to school ahead of me.

I walk alongside him, he buys me a *kaaka*, I put it on my head and run. He runs after me: don't tell your mother, he pants then falls to the ground.

—When I grow up I'm going to be a *kaak* seller.

And the wizened man holds my hand, takes me to school, then goes to work. Take care of yourself. I run into the house but the old man doesn't run after me. *La ilah illa allah.** Bassam is singing in the Land-rover through the pouring rain. I'm not afraid of them, I'm afraid of the cold. Salem, brother, I swear when this war's over, I'll take you on a cruise around the world. It's raining and the sky is flashing with explosions. Voices take on the contours of whispers. But we haven't got enough sand. We must block the street with sand. Bassam dreams of nothing but sand. Why don't we move the entire sea to the barricade? First we bring over the shore and then the waves. She jumped toward the sea. Follow me, she shouted. The waves rose up to her breasts and neck. I could no longer see anything but her brown arms glistening under the rain-specked rays of the sun.

—You're a coward.

—Wait for me, I'll take my clothes off.

—No, come as you are.

I advanced, the waves rose up. I won't marry you, she shouted. She got out of the water, put sand on her clothes and started to run.

—You're a tree.

—I'm Mariam. You don't know Mariam. When I go to Amman, you'll get to know me.

She was running amid the bullets, the bullets getting closer. I must go, I told her. The shooting is getting closer, I must go, she said. The shooting was getting closer,

---

* That is, there is no God but God, part of the *shahada*, the Muslim creed. Often used as an incantation to ward off evil in circumstances of misfortune or to express jubilation.

I stood beside Talal. Nabeel and Salem pressed down the long street and everyone went to his position. Darkness and water. And nothing missing but God's face in his long beard. The rain falling and the street drowning. Standing next to me, he wouldn't answer. Water rising to my waist. Hearing a rustle. The sound of rain and thunder. Nothing'll happen tonight. We can't advance in this rain and darkness. We must wait for Bassam. Maybe he'll manage to bring over the waves and the sea to the position.

Darkness stretching without end. We were just standing. I lit a cigarette, blowing the smoke into the wind. Hearing nothing but the rain rapping against the shacks around us and the sound of quarreling rising out of one of the houses behind. Suddenly, everything lit up, the smell of burning and the sounds of shelling. The sky was flashing and shells were falling everywhere. Fires lighting up and the rain boring into my clothes. I took a deep drag from the cigarette trembling in my hand. It was bitterly cold, and behind me swelled up the sounds of voices and the tumult. A fire on the roof of one of the houses went out suddenly. Three women, in their long *abayahs*, gleaming in the darkness. With their scarves and jangling arms.

—What's that?

Kurdish sorrow was pouring out onto the street. We heard only screams that sounded like cries for help, then the voice receded. Three women splashed through the water, then clambered up the hill behind. I ran toward them.

—Where to?

—To hell. The shelling never hits anything but the houses of the poor.

—Go back home auntie.

—How can I go back? Go on, sonny, and leave us be. God'll provide.

Talal went back to his position. Three women, with children on their shoulders, and water pouring out of water. We could make out the women only with difficulty. They looked like the shadow of the old oil lantern one of them carried.

The commander came running. It looks like they're trying to overrun the street. Get ready. I followed him. I stood at the end of a street leading to the main road where we used to listen for the movement of military vehicles. He took Talal to another street, Talal alone. You've got to get down on the ground, the position commander was saying. He lay down on the water, shivering as it seeped into his body. The shelling was intensifying. We've got to hold our ground. Water mixed with blood. This is the glory of the revolution. You are the pride of the revolution. And the pride of the revolution will stand fast. I was holding my rifle tight and firing. The shots rang in my ears, I couldn't see them. I gripped the hand grenade and threw it. Water splashed up and the shrapnel went flying. The water gasped loudly; this is the glory of the revolution. I was down on the ground. But they weren't advancing. Nothing but an over-powering smell. The smell of rain and brackish water and burning gunpowder. The sound of shells. I couldn't see anything ahead. But Talal stayed down on the ground, shooting, advancing to the main road. Nothing but shelling. The rain was stopping and masonry was beginning to crumble. I looked behind: three women, in their long *abayahs*, running across the steep hill. The first woman sat down on a stone and started to moan quietly. The man approached the woman, took her hand and pulled her up, she stood then fell. The man fell next to her.

—This is the second time. The first time we started to run. They said the others were taking the neighborhood. We fled. Came back to next day. Today, God's wrath has descended upon us. How will we eat?

The hot loaf was on my face.*

—Where did you get that bread from?

He was standing in front of me, holding a steaming cup of coffee.

—God lend you strength. It was a tiring night.

Talal was shouting with joy. Look at the sun. I've bought bread and cheese, and we've got to distribute it. The shelling has to stop. The woman's long robe touched the ground, then swept along beside her. Children threw themselves on it, clutching their heads and wailing.

—What's up, auntie?

—Nothing. I'm looking for my husband. He went out last night saying he was going to buy bread and he hasn't come back. Have you seen any bread? Talal sat among the women, holding the bread. They gathered around him. His voice was rising, sharpening: there's a supply shortage. Have you seen my husband? He went out on the street, said he was going to buy bread. But the bread hasn't come. I put the loaf in my mouth and started chewing. Have you seen any bread, my boy? The woman rushed out of the shack. It's my mother's fault. I told her, Mother, I don't want to get married. My mother died three years ago. She died without a war. How can people die without war. Impossible. Death exists only in war. I put my rifle down. Talal said he was tired, then asked me about our losses. Nothing much, I told him. Only Sameer got a small piece of shrapnel.

The long street that overlooked the church extended forever. Old stores on either side. And the woman piling the clothes in her lap. I drew near; she was crying: have you seen any bread my son?

---

* Because a loaf of Lebanese bread is completely flat and round, it is possible to cover one's face with it.

The shell crashed into the water puddles that were everywhere. The woman ran off. Her robe streaming and her hair tumbling down her face. She went up close to the tank and stood in front of it, her robe draped on the tank. Tank emerging from woman, women emerging from tank.

The man cleared his throat. I'm from the village of Sakhneen. Do you know Sakhneen? The thing is that after we'd attacked the Jewish *kobbaniyyah** several times, we were forced to retreat. The Relief Army** came. You know about the Relief Army, of course. We, however, didn't know about it. My name is Saqr, but in our organization I'm known as Saqr Quraysh. Boy, I tell you, this revolution is beautiful. It's better than previous revolutions. It cares about its dead. In the past, Arab governments didn't care about the dead, or about the living for that matter. Anyway, we got to know the Relief Army. They said the Relief Army would be coming. We waited for it. The women waited, the children waited, and we grew weary. Then all of a sudden we heard shooting in the air. Hurray for the Arabs! And we saw the tank up close. To tell the truth, it was the first time I touched a tank with my own hand. I went up to the tank commander. And after the formal greetings that are, as you know, unavoidable on such occasions, I put my hand on the metal of the tank. Metal is such a pleasure! A tank makes you hold your head high and more. The soldiers stayed in our homes. We hosted them. Three days went by, there they were. Food and drink and their every whim. An army's whims . . . no problem. For it is they who protect our

---

* A corruption of company, the word used by the native Palestinians to designate the early Zionist settlements. The small colonies were assimilated to some kind of compound which might have belonged to a company.

** Also known as the Army of Deliverance (*jaysh al-inqādh*), it was the ill-fitted, poorly trained, army of Arab volunteers formed in 1948 in the last-minute pan-Arab response to what was becoming the inexorable ascendancy of the Zionists in Palestine. It was the first pan-Arab effort to face the Zionist challenge and is a subject of both sadness and derision.

homelands. The homeland cannot be inviolate without an army. And after three days, Abu Sa'eed came to see me. But my good Saqr, the Relief Army isn't relieving anything but its own stomach. What's this army? You must talk to the tank commander. We've slaughtered every last chicken. There isn't a thing left in the village. When does this army fight? Saqr, we'd better take over the *kobbaniyyah* before the Jews take over the country. After much throat-clearing, and greeting and talking, we broached the subject with the tank commander. We're waiting for orders, he told me. Go ahead and attack, I'll answer for it, I said. I can't do that, I'm a volunteer like you, he replied. I'd like to finish with the *kobbaniyyah* before the lot of you. By the end of the argument, the officer had agreed. Truth be told, he was a very energetic sort of officer. He had us assemble in the village square. The tank will move up to the hill and shell the *kobbaniyyah*. Stay in your positions. When the signal to attack is given, move out. I don't want a chaotic battle. Order is fundamental in war. We all agreed; he was a convincing fellow. The tank set off from the square, moving slowly through the village's narrow streets. Then, it disappeared from view. We broke up into groups and took up the positions assigned to us. Then we heard the officer shouting. We ran, and found the tank stuck in the middle of a narrow street, unable to move any farther. The officer began to curse. The hell with this war, how are we expected to fight without roads? We got picks and shovels, and began digging to widen the road. And after three days of hard labor, the tank managed to move, to our *la ilah illal allah*'s and *allahu akbar*'s. At any rate, the thing is that the tank fired just two shells and the cannon jammed. Sir, why don't we just attack? Ask the good Lord, he snapped back. Anyway, the Jews attacked from their *kobbaniyyah* before we could launch our attack. We went to the officer. What do we do?

I can't do a thing. I'm going to beat a retreat. The cannon has broken down and a tank without a cannon is useless. And in any case, it's a lost battle. Anyhow, the Arab armies will soon be here and will liberate Palestine. Retreat with me now. Then we'll come back, no problem. We agreed. No. Some of us agreed. I swear *I* didn't agree, and neither did Abu Sa'eed. We fought. What else could we do? They attacked with around twenty tanks. What could I do? We retreated and surrendered our fate to God, after many people had died. Actually, we buried the dead before coming to Lebanon.

She stepped back from the tank, put her scarf on and waved, signaling she was going. Naturally, I didn't ask where to. The shells were dropping randomly and we had to stay put. The woman went without my knowing what had happend to her husband.

—We've got hold of a tank.
—What's this?

A genuine tank, with Nabeel driving it. The soldiers surrendered; they said they didn't want to fight their brothers. I asked them to stay with us but they left. Said they would come back. The tank took off and we walked along behind it. I want a tank made of all colors. Do you know colors, says the young African boy. I don't know them, I don't know what colors mean. Everything is as colored as it can be. And Talal wants a colored tank. The guys brought over lots of colors and began to paint the tank. It refused to budge and we painted its body every possible color. I want a red tank because the revolution has started. The smell of gunpowder everywhere. Beirut has acquired a small of its own. In the past, I couldn't make our Beirut's smell. Nobody knew it had a smell. Everyone smelled his own smell, or the waiter's smell, a mixture of alcohol and cheap cologne.

But now Beirut has a definite smell. Everywhere there is gundpowder and empty streets inhabited only by the mist and the sound of the shells and of the Korean rockets barking in the air. Stench and barking.

—And what happened to the woman after that?

—I don't know.

We took the tank and colored it. We took off the 500mm. machine gun and fixed it down in the church. The neighborhood kids gathered around the tank. They drove it, then it stopped. We tied a clothesline to the cannon from the window. The clothes hung out were of every color. Talal held the loaf, I don't know what we should do. The revolution should start. But it has started, Salem said. You don't understand what the revolution is. This is revolution. Revolutions are like this. Do you know why a loaf is round? Because it's a loaf. A loaf can't be any different, just like a cemetery. A cemetery is round but we can't see that from the inside. Everything's like that. We only see the surface of things. The smell of gunpowder was spreading. Carrying our guns, we were standing in the winter sun, relaxed. Scattered bursts of shooting.

A man approached. You don't know 'Ammiq. You eat grapes and drink 'araq but you don't know 'Ammiq. Now, there's grapes. My father's a hard-headed man. You don't know the way, come on, I served in Beirut, I know all her streets. But the mountains are prettier. The sight of grapes dangling from the vine whets my appetite for 'araq. You don't drink 'araq—that's a mistake. 'Araq is very important. It's fire. 'Araq inside me and I'm on fire. Human beings should burn up. 'Araq alone sets you alight. I put away some 'araq inside me and go pilfering. Do you know what I did? After all that had happened, I finally realized that the government was falling apart. I took the armored car I was in charge of driving and went off with it. That was before everything really collapsed. I fled alone with the APC from Hawsh al-Umara to 'Ammiq. My father came out of the house, showed no surprise. He took the APC and leashed it in front of the house. I got up in the morning and couldn't find it. I must go and join the revolution in the APC. I asked my mother, she said my father took the APC and went down to the vineyard. I ran to the vineyard and saw him trying to fix metal farm attachments to it. I'm going to plow. By God, this APC's better than a tractor. The APC became the talk of the village. The *mukhtar** came by to congratulate us and proposed that an agricultural cooperative be set up. But, *Mukhtar*, you've been plowing your lands with tractors for ages and we've not asked you to set up cooperatives. The tractor is private property but the APC is public property. That's what the *mukhtar* who knows about these things said. We argued and shouted at each other; it seemed as if things wouldn't be resolved peacefully. *Mukhtar*, there isn't any such thing as private property anymore. Anything goes. Everything's topsy-turvy. But the *mukhtar* wanted to take the APC and my father wanted to hold onto it. To avoid trouble, I stole the APC back from in front of the house and returned it to the barracks. It was all over; nobody was going to ride anyone roughshod from now on. That's what they told us. But fighting in cities is a hard thing. It takes a tremendous effort to kill your enemy. This isn't war. I don't know. You might be right. But everything's fallen apart.

The Kurdish woman asking after her husband, her husband stretched out cold in the middle of the street.
— He's going to rot there in the street.
— We'll wait for nightfall then drag him off. Don't mention it.

---

* A village or town headman or mayor.

She bent down. She was holding a loaf. She bit into it. May God repay you. But don't forget me.

—We won't forget you.

And he—he was stretched out on his stomach, his legs raised slightly off the ground, the ground wet with mud, sand and dust all around him.

* * *

"What is it you were doing in the ancient garden three hundred years ago."

The mountain was full of holes but it edged along. The women were standing in two long lines waiting for the war. But the war wouldn't come. We've been waiting for the war for three hundred years. But the war always comes with two large holes in it: one, above, out of which the woman's neck rises, strangulated, and one in the middle before we are born. The advancing mountain was full of holes, like the war. The mountain's just like the war, I told him, my voice rolling down between our feet which stumbled through the night-filled village with its strange silence and cold wind. We reached the forest. An old abandoned house, pine trees. Making a fire inside a pile of stones so that no one would see it.

—Do you see the trees? The people's war has started. A people's war needs trees. For Vietnam's sake, at least.

Jungles and swamps. Trees and the embers of a fire that has begun to die out. For fifty years now we've known nothing but wars.

—That's not important, Talal was saying. Look at the mountains. This is the first time we go up to the mountains. Nabeel was dreaming of sand. I don't like mountains.

—Why did you come then?

— Duty. Then he smiled. War in Beirut is nicer.

— Swamps and mosquitoes. You like swamps.

— I like the city.

I like women, Talal said. Tonight, we'll move on from the glory of the revolution, to the glory of death. Death is a tranquil state. In the middle of the shooting, the explosions and the noise, leaping and bounding, you subside into stillness, complete stillness.

But the mountain was full of holes.

A woman standing, holding piles of food, surrounded by men and women. We saw the fire so we brought over some food. The woman put the food down and went. We ate. The food stuck in my throat. I must puncture my neck and then I'll become a mountain.

The mountain was king. Sanneen was king. But who could climb such a barren mountain? Impossible to move such gear without mules. The mule was the real king. We went up. We carried the ammunition up on a mule, following behind it as it led us to the top. Snow. Fog. And the red shots piercing the night. Talal bent down, put on his glasses. Three hundred years ago the lithe young boy was a leaf lying on a shore. A passer-by picked it up and put it in his pocket. The Chinese seer bided his time. The man didn't know that things lie in wait. The Chinese seer took the leaf and spoke. The man didn't understand. And when he came back to ask, he found that the seer had died. That the rice which used to grow in the street had become a fiery alcohol. But the young African boy climbs my neck. He doesn't talk, doesn't ask me. He dreams that he won't travel, but he will. Next to me slept a tall man with a thick beard. He put his hands behind his head and slept amid the drops of water dripping from the roof of the tent and the snow-covered snow.

—Come on, let's go light a fire at the top. The top of the mountain must go up in flames. What'd happen? A few shells . . . no problem.

He lit a fire. Raised his arms. Took off his khaki shirt and waved it in the air.

Here, the quail sleeps. Here, the quail dies, said one of the fighters in his unerring village accent. They stake out the quail and then kill it. The mule was bleeding. It was hit by a piece of shrapnel in the midriff. Its eyes cast down, not moaning, just letting the blood run down its belly without stirring. The mule was king. Sanneen was grayish. Snow, gray patches and incalculable expanses. We're higher than the clouds, said the man with the thick beard, holding a piece of canned meat and chewing it as though it were chocolate. One must eat. Tomorrow, you'll eat like me. I'm a married man. That means I'm a practical man. I understand things. I know a woman is never pleased. If you make love to her, she gets fed up with so much love-making. And if you don't make love to her, she asks what the point of marriage is. My wife, whom I left a thousand years ago, doesn't understand. She thinks I'm not serious. But the matter's settled. I'm standing on the highest peak of the highest mountain and making up my mind, once and for all, that this wife who's just like all wives isn't fit for marriage. Don't look at me like that. Eating is inevitable. You can't withstand the cold without hormones and vitamins. There isn't any bread. The bread has spoiled. It got soggy with snow and has become like a lump of mud. One can't eat mud and one can't mix meat and snow.

On the peak, where everything is just like everything else. There were thirty men, sleeping in the snow. Their rifles slung around their necks, gazing into each other's faces. Asking questions. Nabeel jumping up and down. The football player jumping up and down to escape the cold. The shells flying about lighting up the snow. Planes piercing the clouds once in a while, but still remote. Because the mountain had become remote.

The man with the thick beard called Nazeeh propped himself up on his left elbow, stretched out on a woolen blanket placed on patches of snow and the gray earth. I'm tired, he said. No, the war is tiring, but it's not like women. Why do people usually associate war with women? Movies are dumb. In films, there must always be wars and, alongside them, women. They even put in a woman with Che Guevara. And the hero always dies while the woman survives to mourn him. Of course, my wife will cry. She's like all wives, so she will cry. But even death, which is *the* question of all questions, isn't a problem. It's a trivial question that comes up in times of illness. When a man is sick, his head fills up with problems and he begins asking questions. But when he's as strong as a mule, he behaves with the simplicity of one.

Talal was standing beside me chewing cold tinned broad beans in an attempt to still his hunger.

— Why are you talking about death and women? You should be talking about victory.

Victory is a tattered robe, Nazeeh would say. Do you see those clouds close by? You can reach up and touch them, but you can't hold onto them. That's what we're like. We can touch victory but we can't hold onto it.

The gunfire sparked above our heads, then the shells began to sound that faint whining which is pulverized by the noise of their crashing to the ground. Debris was flying over our heads while Sameer, with his beard and his tenderness, leaped gaily, firing, tumbling down through the rocks. I can't see a thing. This fog is thick, he screamed. But Nabeel didn't answer. He was on his knees, firing tensely, the curses preceding the bursts of gunfire. For his part, Nazeeh was sprawled out on the snow, relaxed, firing calmly, looking to his right and seeing Talal, nerves taut, fighting like someone praying in a church. Suddenly, the shooting stopped. Sa'eed came running. They've run away and left this. He had an automatic rifle magazine in his hand. This kind of war isn't enough, Sameer said.

— What would you suggest?

— We should stone them. A rifle's a rifle, but a stone is part of my hand. I should feel that it's my hand that does the fighting, and not this cold metal which doesn't satisfy the need.

Talal smiled. This mountain has turned you into a savage.

Thirty men standing on the mountaintop, lighting a fire and dancing. Eating canned meat. Seeking refuge in their memories. We must stop talking about memories, Salem said. We are making the future, memories don't make the future, memories fuse into ballads and songs. Ahmed's voice rising, splitting through the rocks, floating into the cold winds. I'm king of the mountain, Ahmed was saying.

— We're insects thrown into this vast expanse. Mountains . . . as we climb them, we become little.

— That's a lie. We get bigger and the mountain becomes little. That's what they always say: Man in Nature is like a tiny insect. But it isn't true.

— I've grown taller, said Salem.

— I'm the tallest man in the world, said Sameer.

— *We* are the real kings, said Talal. But we share the throne with these two mules.

The lithe young African boy was running. Slow down a bit, I told her. But she ran on, the sand flying up from her bare feet. She dropped to the ground. I'm going to put you in a little box and put the little box in my pocket. Because you don't deserve any better. She laughed. I don't like prisoners.

— And I don't like prisoners either, but I'm forced to.

— Forced! That's what all tyrants say; when the truth embarrasses them, they start telling you the story of their troubles and it boils down to their being forced to be tyrannical. You're just like them.

My foot was getting bigger, the snow lined my shoes. Look, said Talal. The colors of the rainbow spilling into one another. All the colors that I've ever seen and those I've never seen. The mountain opens its mouth and the sun tumbles out. A mountain rolling through the clouds. The colors resemble the sea but the sea is flat. Colors forming circular gaps. My hand reaching out, catching nothing. The perforated mountain moves. We run toward the valley. The valley embraces my body, cuts it in two halves, and the distant sea enters the clouds. I raise my hand to my face. My face is a big, wizened apple. And my hand rises toward the sun that falls into our eyes as it tumbles between the flames and the mouth of the whale that is about to swallow it.

The villager-fighter carried his shoes and walked barefoot. Yesterday, the sun burned us; today, the fog and the rain have come and taken the sun to the bottom of the valley. But the problem is these damned shoes. They stay wet. I walk as though I were carrying the mountain in my leg. My toes are so swollen I can't feel them anymore. Snow is against war. He carried his shoes and entered something like a tent. Water everywhere. The smell of sodden wool is like the smell of sheep before their slaughter. By God, it's the butcher that's king. What does he care? He does whatever he pleases. Slaughtering and selling, he can eat until doomsday.

What kind of food rations are these?

My tongue was dry and my insides burned. I went into the tent and found the villager-fighter talking politics with Nazeeh. Propped up on his left hand, Nazeeh was shivering with cold. His face was red with sun and fog. His raised right hand gesticulated as he talked on and on.

The Eastern Question must be settled once and for all. For three hundred years now the West has been driving the knife into our side in the name of the Eastern Question and the rights of minorities. We should be done with the question for good.

I sat next to them and listened. Then the discussion began to heat up. The villager-fighter's voice rose. I looked at him, he was holding an orange which glowed in the dark tent. The orange took part in the debate in its own way, shifting in slow motion from left hand to right. As the argument flared and abated, the orange would step in to cut the silence in a quick sleight-of-hand as if he had become a trickster who puts an orange in his ear and has a tree come out of his mouth. He put the orange on top of the sodden blankets all squashed together. Nazeeh leaned over and reached out but the villager's hand was quicker. He grabbed the orange, it danced between his hands, then he let it roll a little.

—But where did the orange come from?

He ignored the question. Then his voice took on a special inflection.

—Weapons have to be cared for in this climate. Water seeps into them. The important thing's to keep on fighting. That's what you want. I agree. Provided that we don't stay up here on the mountaintop in this unbearable cold. The orange rolled away. Talal grabbed it. The villag-er-fighter leaped to his feet.

—I want the orange. It's my own private orange.

—There's no private property in the revolution.

He pounced, grasped the orange and wrenched it out of my hand, and sat in a corner of the tent all by him-self with his orange. We advanced on him. He put the orange behind his back.

—We should go to Baskinta. We'd find houses and things to eat there.

The sky flashed with the sound of distant rifles. Nazeeh stood up. The battle has begun. We should eat this orange before the battle, split it between the three of us. Talal rose to his feet and grabbed his rifle. The villager-fighter slipped the orange into his pocket and began trying to put his shoes on. We were all set. But the orange had escaped. He disappeared and then came back, smelling of orange. Reeking of orange from head to toe.

—What happened to the orange?

—The orange turned into a tree. The man has become a tree.

They were in front of us but they weren't like humans. Of course, they were ordinary men. But no. We opened fire, they fell theatrically. I couldn't see properly. But they were falling. It was going into slow motion. A man falling as though he were play-acting. I'm not sure it's man. We've done an excellent job. No one can take this moun-tain. We are the guardians of the snow and the cold. But I don't know, maybe that wasn't clearly understood. I'm sure of it, killing is something else. Here, it's as if I were shoot-ing at stones. Actually, I was shooting at targets, mere tar-gets. And the targets behaved like targets. That's all there is to it . . .

Talal took off his glasses, wiping away the mud mixed with sweat. Nazeeh came. The tree has died. The villager-fighter, with his oversized shoes, and his face burned with snow and fog, approached, slung across a mule. Asleep, with three men leading the white mule holding onto him.

The mule stopped in front of me. Talal bent down. The smell of death is like the smell of oranges. Death is an orange tree. When I die I want to smell like an orange tree.

We returned to the tent. Talal went to the villager-fighter's bag. He opened it.

—Look, another orange was waiting for the end of the battle.

Nazeeh took the orange, divided into two, took half and squeezed it, the drops trickling into his mouth and onto his beard.

—A toast to the martyrs. Why don't you have some?

—I can't.

—You're a romantic. Don't you want to smell like a tree?

I put the orange in my mouth. It tasted really sharp. I ate it without peeling it, all of it. The tent began to smell like the vast orange grove stretching from Saida to the end of the world.

* * *

The last option is me, I told her, our footsteps striking the streets of the dark town. Clothes rustling, words spoken in silence. Cruising ahead of us, a Land-rover filled with ammunition and food. Walking along, whispering to each other and listening to the whispers of the villagers gazing at us in awe. Pleased with ourselves, full of pride, just as we used to dream we would be when we were little. We are little but we are just as proud as we should be.

A long line of fighters who've come from everywhere to the wedding that hasn't started. We filed into the seraglio. They said it, alone, could fit the hundreds of *fedayeen* that've come from all over. Candle-lights, long corridors. We moved in and on in, not understanding where we were. We found ourselves in a very large, long room with high windows fenced off with barbed wire.

—We're in the prison. We came to fight and find ourselves in prison. On principle, I don't agree. We can't sleep in the prison, even if it is empty. No way—even if we abolish prisons. A *feda'i* can't sleep in prison. That's a matter of principle. I'm not about to agree to it.

Salem, B-7 rocket-launcher in hand, his face trembling against the prison wall, his voice raised: I will not sleep in prison. I came to fight and I won't sleep here.

Talal walked up to the circle gathering around Salem. Standing like a lecturer, speaking unhurriedly: this isn't a matter of principle, it's a practical matter. There isn't a place big enough for us other than this prison. Besides, this is magnificent. Imagine—emerging from the prison to destroy all prisons. Revolution beginning from the prison. I don't think this thing was planned but it's happening as if it were. It's as if it were saying that it's prison which will destroy all prisons.

You're a romantic, I told him.

I'm a romantic, he answered me.

The mountains that stretched away stretched on and on. We must get to know the area really well, said Nabeel.

The debate expanded. Small groups forming, distributed about the corners and the corridors. The wan light paling further. The shells merging with sleepiness. Then, by around nine o'clock, the entire hall was asleep. Candles asleep, I asleep and Talal asleep beside me. Even the shells seemed to want to sleep. Talal woke me up.

— Do you know why we're falling asleep so quickly?

— Fatigue, I said to him, my voice jumbled with yawning and drowsiness.

— No, it's not fatigue. It's prison. Prison means sleep. Lots of little problems, then you escape into sleep. When you sleep, you can disregard all prohibitions. You escape to something that is yours alone. Sleep is mine alone. No one can share it with me. I sleep as I please. I dream. Toss and turn. That's why we sleep and why prisoners sleep.

— But I'm not a prisoner.

— Of course, we'll destroy the prisons. But in order to destroy the prisons we had to go to prison.

— I want to sleep. And anyway, you're contradicting yourself.

— That's life. Contradiction doesn't mean that I'm contradicting myself. Contradiction means contradiction.

— And sleep means sleep.

I turned my back toward him and tried to sleep. But Talal wouldn't sleep. My father says the fish in the sea don't sleep. I've never asked him where then do the fish sleep? My father insists that fish don't sleep. And Talal wouldn't sleep. And my hand wouldn't reach the prison's high ceiling. I got up. Red flames were glowing through the small high windows. My feet dragged on the tiles covered with the dry woolen blankets. In the side room, voices and mumbling. I approached and watched them from behind the bars. Four men, each sitting by himself in a dark corner. A single, quivering candle. I went up to the bars. One of them came toward me, then the others moved. The first one opened his mouth, then the others did the same. Only one voice emerged, in differing gradations, as if we'd been in a

Greek drama. I don't understand, I said to them. I'm a prisoner, one of them said.

—And I'm a prisoner like you.

—But you're carrying an automatic rifle.

—Tomorrow, I'll give you one.

One of them drew back, crestfallen.

—You're making fun of us.

—I'm not making fun of you. I mean it. Tomorrow, I'll give you weapons. But why? Why are you here?

—It's a bit complicated. They said they were worried about me. I'm from a remote village, and you know what the atmosphere's like there.

Talal and Nabeel and some others came. Talal seemed concerned.

—Look, tomorrow, I'll take you to your village. There are no prisoners here. We've abolished prisons once and for all.

—Tomorrow, I'll give you a rifle and you'll come and fight with us. Do you accept?

—But I know nothing about fighting.

—You'll learn to fight as you're fighting. Are you scared?

—Of course he's scared. I'm scared. We're all scared. Courage is a fallacy. There's no such thing as courage. Fear comes before or after. We're always scared, whether before or after. We're scared of prison before going there. We're scared of death before dying. We're scared of war after the battle starts. We're scared of women before getting married.

—No. We're scared of women after getting married.

The prisoners huddled around the prisoner who was scared, and we gathered around Nabeel who wouldn't scare. In the end, we had to sleep. The sound of shells grew around the prison as my sadness grew. Talal grew sad and his sadness clouded the three prison days we spent waiting for the release of the prisoners. Talal in a corner, counting the shells and waiting for his turn. Then the unit commander came and told us we were going back because the operation had been canceled. But what shall we do with the prisoners? Talal asked. The commander said it was a complicated matter, needing time and contacts. We can't act on our own. We'll leave them for the time being. They'll no doubt be released in the end.

Everything is temporary, she said, holding her picture. Look at my picture. You're prettier than the picture. Talal lifted the camera to his shoulder. The lithe young African boy ascended, blending into the sand and the raindrops.

—I'm talking because I'm sad. We're dying like flies. Ever since the Mongols, maybe just before or after them, we've been dying like flies. Dying without thinking. Dying of disease, of bilharzia, of the plague, in childbirth or the absence of childbirth. We're dying like flies. Without any consciousness, without dignity, without anything.

—And yet you call for war. And war means the death of even more people.

—Revolution means life.

—But they're dying.

—They're dying with consciousness. Consciousness is the opposite of death.

We can abolish death only with consciousness. Then we'll be over with dying like flies and start into real death.

—Death abolishes consciousness. Death abolishes consciousness, do you hear?

She ran, put sand on her hair and began shaking her head.

—You're a bourgeoise and I don't love you.

She ran off and I didn't run after her. I carried my shoes in my hand and slowly walked to the car. Where to? she yelled. Aren't you going to take me prisoner and put me in the box? I opened the car door, turned on the ignition and left.

* * *

The snow was rolling over our heads. Fog, and the big mountain bowing at our feet. The enemy was advancing—trying to advance—but we stood at the top, immovable, as gods. We were advancing slowly and the white mules slowly advanced with us. The sound of gunfire fusing into our voices. Swollen, our feet had become gray splotches, part of the snow. We ourselves remained. Going back over our memories. Recounting the prison story. Remembering the four prisoners. Each one telling the story the way he liked, the way he remembered it, or the way it was. Shots rang out in the vast expanse where the sun was rolling, the snow falling, and colors didn't look like colors. My throat was dry, my hand wooden around the rifle. We were listening to their voices. They were cursing and we were cursing back and opening fire. We need Sameer's stones, Nazeeh shouted. Moments later, they retreated. We were sitting quietly around our rifles when Salem jumped up, yelling, his voice booming like the mountains: who's there? He ran toward a man, whom at first glance I thought was one of our comrades.

—Who are you?

Talal ran, Nazeeh ran. They took his rifle.

—Who are you?

His voice was trembling. He spoke without having to say a single word.

—Who are you?

—A shepherd.

—And the rifle?

—I'm lost.

Nazeeh shouted, a prisoner, hold him fast. Tie him up with rope. He stepped forward and hit him in the face. Welcome Mr. Fascist, the message has been received. Don't hit him, Salem yelled. Talal came running, grabbed him by the arm, come on.

I'm a student, he said. We're the new shift. They left me on the mountain. Don't kill me.

He was trembling, as prisoners do, Nazeeh was trembling, as conquerors do, and Talal trembled. I held the prisoner by the right arm and Talal held him. We took him to the tent, gave him a glass of hot tea. What happened to the four prisoners, Talal asked me. Nabeel came, we should kill him on the spot. Sons of bitches. Fascists!

The prisoner quaked. We're not going to kill him, said Talal. He's poor, just like us.

—Why is he fighting on their side?

—When will the poor fight their own wars?

—There's no war that's special to the poor. Buildings must tear down buildings, and shacks buildings and cities cities. And out of the destruction will rise the poor's special war.

Talal sat beside the prisoner and started talking. He told him about the South, about the poor in Nabaa, about Tall al-Zaatar.* He told him that Amman had been ablaze, that the orange hadn't died. He told him the story of the prison and of our friendship with the four prisoners. The

---

* The former was a run-down area for poor migrant workers who constituted Beirut's lumpen-proletariat in the "boom" years of the '60s and '70s; it was situated on the outskirts of what is now East Beirut, not far from Qarantina and Maslakh. Tall al-Zaatar was a Palestinian refugee camp, also in an outlying area of East Beirut, which was besieged for months in the first year of the war in Lebanon; it finally fell in a fierce battle in the summer of 1976.

prisoner was convinced. Prisoners are always easily convinced.

—But why are you fighting with them?

Don't kill me, I beg you, the prisoner says. We won't kill you, Talal says. But talk. I'm convinced, the prisoner says. Always, prisoners are convinced easily. And prisoners die easily.

* * *

The last option is me, I told her. The last option is death, says Nazeeh, walking behind the white mule which stumbles as it makes its way across the rugged hills. And Talal sleeps quietly, swaying on the mule's back. One bullet in the head. Drops of blood fall, trickling onto the mule's white belly. The last option is death, he said to her. The four prisoners, they're still dreaming of rifles. And the mountain trembles under our footfalls. The last option is death, I tell her. The loaf goes dry in my hand. Talal sleeps, surrendering like a real king. And Sanneen doesn't answer.

Chapter 4

The
STAIRS

1

The woman drops down from the ceiling. My eyes cling to
the feet. A woman dangling from the ceiling. I no longer
understand anything. Really, I no longer understand a
thing. I've been afraid of the ceiling for years. The ceiling
is low. Buildings are high and ceilings are low. I used to tell
my wife I was afraid of low ceilings. But she's a modern
woman; she likes modern buildings and won't live in the village. And what will happen to our children, I tell her. Nothing, she answers. They'll live in nice modern houses, not
like this house, mangy as your bald patch. But they'll live
in even more run-down houses and become like rats. A
modern woman is right. And I too am a modern man and
am right. I bought the car and used to drive it the way other
men do, my wife by my side and the children, looking like
domesticated animals, in the back. And then we all like
modern things. Beyond that, I don't know. But the woman's
dangling from the ceiling as if she were falling. No, she's not
falling. I'm standing still, I can hear voices, I'm trying to
make out the meanings of the words. But I can't. Yet, we
should understand things precisely. I no longer understand

this "precisely" in spite of the fact that I'm a law-and-order man and all for the police. Crazy Hani, what's he doing now in the grave? At least, he's not asking questions and his eyes don't wander off when he's talking. His eyes were remote as two drops of water. The physics teacher always talked about the drop of water and I never understood what he meant until I looked at this man's eyes. Two, circular, depthless drops of water. He would disappear into his eyes when he talked and stay there, transformed into two drops of water, and curse the police and the state. I'd stand beside him and say nothing. What would I say? There's no police now, Hani's dead and the situation isn't any better. And this woman's dangling from the ceiling. Her leg is white and her thigh is white. No, not white. Something like white. And her foot's as big as a man stuck to the wall. I go up to the wall and press my body to it. But the man is moving, he's shaking. The whole room's shaking. My hand is shaking and the white liquid spilling onto the ground. I put a bit of water in my mouth but don't swallow; I hold it, letting my right cheek swell. I go up to the chair and try to lean against it. But the shadows, the shadows are swaying as if we were inside a city made of thick cardboard. Colors dark and things receding. My hand drops but I try. I'm really trying. I stand in front of the woman who looks like a thick rope. I extend my hand toward the rope. I hear a scream, step back a little. I brace my back against the wall. The wall shakes. I feel the wall is about to fall on my face, it can't stand upright. I see the cupboard and smile. You can't but smile when you see the cupboard. My aunt loved that cupboard. When she died, the first thing I did was to go to the cupboard and weep in front of its doors. What can a woman do? A woman who spent her life in her brother's house, sweeping, washing dishes, and feeling like an outsider. She used to cry. She'd tell me about the young suitor whom my father rejected because he was crazy and didn't love her. I know the truth, my aunt would say. He was a drunkard, played around with chicks, and then got drunk out of his mind. Your father was always getting drunk. When the suitor visited him to ask for my hand in marriage, he was drunk, and he advised him not to marry me because I'm ugly. When the man insisted, my brother cursed him and told him not to marry because marriage is a calamity and threw him out of the house. And then he came to me, told me, apologized and started to cry. I said nothing. My aunt would cry and look at the cupboard. The best thing's the cupboard. It doesn't feel anything, she'd hit it, my aunt would hit the cupboard violently, but it wouldn't cry because it didn't feel anything. My aunt would cry. I want to become a cupboard. I'd sit beside her and cry. Then I thought of becoming a cupboard. The woman dangling from the ceiling contorts herself like a circus woman. I met my wife many years ago. A million years ago. When I got married, I told my father that the first woman resembles the last. He laughed then looked at his wife; she smiled. It was the first time I felt that my mother was the wife of this loathsome man. They fool around in bed together, then he beats her while making love to her to heighten his pleasure. I used to think that I couldn't lie next to a woman on the same bed without making love to her the whole night long. How could I fall asleep while a woman, a complete woman slept beside me. My eyelids wouldn't so much as blink when I used to put a picture of a naked woman next to me in bed. I'd stay wide awake, me and the picture and other things. Then I'd get out of bed, fold the picture carefully, put it inside the book and sleep. But now, a million years later, I sleep with her beside me without folding her away or putting her into a book. Of course, I don't know. My father's laugh, and his glance at his wife, are still in my mind. I know nothing about women save the last woman who's called my wife and who loves me the way she loves cake. As for the first woman, and the second and the third, they're still in the magazines that I started to buy on the sly and looked at or read at the office. Until a colleague caught me. He stole the magazine from my drawer and went around to the secretaries with it. I was so embarrassed my bald patch blushed. I felt my head ablaze with blood. From that day on, I became shy of the secretaries and their impertinent looks and laughs. As for the men, they would whisper among themselves.

The glass was swaying in my hand as if it wanted to fall. The white liquid had a pungent smell and darkness was falling slowly. That's the way darkness comes. You think it's coming down slow, then suddenly without you feeling a thing you fall into darkness and turn on the lights. But in these black days, there's neither electricity nor anyone who turns lights on for that matter. Everything was quivering. Even the stars are only seen quivering in this cursed city called Beirut. The heat is stifling. The sound of gunfire coming over distantly. How can they fight in such heat? How can they not just sleep on top of the sandbags? It's impossible. The noise heats the air even further. And of course, the dust from the shells fills the air with clouds. So it's raining in summer. Yesterday there was rain. Hot air with rain. Like in miracles. The sky's sweating, my wife said, thinking she was being witty. But it's God's wrath. How can they? I don't know. These new shells that howl like wolves. But best of all is this yarn about Vietnam. They want a new Vietnam! There'll only be wars afterward. War means Vietnam and to have Vietnam you need a war. And Hani is content. I don't understand this man. Poor thing, he died. My wife cried, as all women do, when he died. But me, I didn't cry. I couldn't cry over that man. Then they told me he died by mistake. No, I figured as much. They said he was out getting supplies when this shell came and killed him. That's a mistake in my view. He shouldn't have been getting supplies. Even in war, we don't know how to arrange death. But he held the stick by the end. He'd say: you can't hold a stick by the middle. Anyone who holds a stick by the middle can't fight. If you held the stick by the middle . . . here, his face would go red as a tomato and his eyes would wander off, and you discovered that this man had turned into two drops of water . . . and the enemy attacked, how would you fight? The stick would then be against you. You'd have to put the stick up your arse and surrender or get killed. He went and held it by the end, but he died. He, too, died. Whichever way we hold the stick we're going to die. That is the wisdom I have arrived at. And then, there are things one can't hold by the end. How do you make love to a woman? You've got to hold her by the middle, to hold her tight, then you do it to her. The middle is sex and sex is life. So where's the wrong and where's the right and where's life?

The voices were growing louder and there was the shuffle of feet and of the wooden clogs that have become the fashion these days. Wooden clogs suit women. But people forget. They forget everything and think only of bread. I, too, forget but the bread doesn't forget a thing. There's bread in the streets. I don't know why I dreamed and why I did that. I woke up in the morning, smiling. We'd been sleeping in a shelter crammed with people and smells. The women's voices buzzed all night as if we'd been condemned to listen without being able to object. The loaves, white as nurses' coats, were piled on the pavements. My daughter and I stood amid thousands of people who'd come from everywhere and started to eat the bread, putting it in little bags and going off. My daughter laughed and pointed to a white loaf. But the crush of people prevented me from reaching the pavement where there was all the bread in the world. Abu Issam was shouting at the top of his voice, the bread turning into white froth around his lips. He tried to stop the crush of people advancing. My little daughter's tears flowed white, the color of the loaves. And I just stood there, unable to move forward. When I opened my eyes, inside the shelter, my daughter was in her mother's lap and Abu Issam was shouting and cursing his wife. Then he got up. I went with him to the bakery, where there were thousands of people. But the black bread was in plastic bags and people were shouting to the sound of the distant explosions and the nearby shooting. Everything that's happened and hasn't happened was there on the face of the baker, taking the banknotes, crumpling them up and putting them in the drawer all the while cursing the electricity, the water, and the impossibility of working under such conditions. By the time I got back home, the sun was high in the middle of the sky, the smell of cooking filled the house, my wife was beating the children and there wasn't enough bread, and reading the papers was forbidden.

— You waste all your money on newspapers and then you spend your time listening to the radio. Since you listen to the radio, what are the papers for?

Women don't understand politics. You can't convince a woman that what's happening is important, that our fate hangs in the balance.

— But you sit at home all day.

But she doesn't understand. The truth is I can't . . . At work, I used to feel I was part of something, of the institution. But now, I don't even feel I'm part of my wife. There's nothing left but noise. Hearing is the only sense that has any meaning. Everything else is meaningless. Hani didn't agree. God exists, it's inevitable. I'm a believer, but I can't. Even faith has become an object of ridicule for my wife. Stop getting drunk then I'll listen to you. She doesn't give due consideration to my circumstances. Ever since I've stopped going to work, I've felt oppressed. The newspaper I read oppresses me. The black letters flow over my face and clothes.

— Don't leave the papers lying around in front of the children, my wife screams. Why don't you throw them away? You pile them up in the house, the children play with them and the house stinks of ink.

Even reading the papers is forbidden now. She does whatever she pleases. She chatters all day and cries all night and she's afraid. This modern woman, who when I married her I thought I was marrying the 20th century, is worse than my mother. And I bow down before her like a he-goat who's had his horns cut off. My father laughed before he died; I laughed when he died. Our customs are incomprehensible. A man dies, they lay him out on a bed; then the women gather round, douse his corpse with cologne and begin their lamentations and wailing. My father laughs and whispers in my ear. Really, they wait for a man to die then they have this sexual celebration right there in front of his corpse. Wouldn't it be better if they gathered around him while he was alive? When my father died, I couldn't conceal my mirth. He was at the center of the sexual celebration in an old neck-tie my mother got him God alone knows where, cologne all over — and under — him, and the woman ululating. As soon as I entered, the wailing intensified and I burst out laughing. The women stopped crying and looked at one another. And my mother, she started quivering with embarrassment and muttering unintelligibly. Then the wailing resumed, my father neither speaking nor moving.

The ceiling from which the woman dangles is moving closer to my head. Things are purple and the candle's white. But the candle has a smell. The ceiling's getting closer. And the white liquid is trickling down from my hand onto the floor and the smell is spreading. Salt doesn't have a smell. The air was stifling. They said they could. Of course, I didn't believe it. I have no faith in superstition and magic. But it danced. The small table hovered in the air and danced. They shut the doors and windows. We were sweating as if we'd been in a Turkish bath. Speak. I looked and saw the small table flying through the air. It was small, the size of a hand, but it flew. I was very frightened. They said they'd try the glass; the spirit of the dead would come, enter the glass, move among the letters, and tell all. I told my wife when I got back home that I was afraid. I was surprised by her sudden enthusiasm and her desire to be acquainted with every detail. I can't, I told her. She made fun of me. I didn't tell her that I'd turned down their offer to conjure up the spirit of one of my friends. Hani was before me. I saw him, full-bodied and tall. But I was scared by him. I came home running. The streets were full of darkness and fear and my mouth was salty. The dead and the living coexist in a remarkable way in this city. The dead have become more numerous than the living. I slept all night, at home. I told my wife I felt I was suffocating so I wouldn't go down to the shelter. I begged her to stay beside me.

—And the children, what shall I do with them? What if a shell hits the house?

Anyway, she left me there and went down to the shelter with the children. I stayed alone, with the sound of the shells and the darkness. I said to myself, I'll sleep in my own bed, it's allright. But the shells whistled as though they were coming out of my ears. I got up and sat in the corridor. I said to myself, I'll sleep sitting up. My body ducked with every shell, incoming and outgoing. I spent quite a unique sort of night. I wished I were a little child. Even our fantasies have become ridiculous. I slept sitting up, then awoke in the morning to a tremendous clamor. I don't know what happened exactly, but the shell fell near the house.

I put the glass down on the table. Took the white candle and tried to put it down on the table. But it fell from my hand. I bent down, the floor was dirty and the candle light slanted off to the right. I took hold of it a second time and approached the woman dangling from the ceiling. She was screaming. I looked carefully: my wife's face was white as she groped for something to clutch onto. Then, all of a sudden, I heard a terrible crash, and the ground was covered with glass. It was tiny and glittered in the candle light and my smell spread all over the house. I heard my wife scream. Then she dropped from the ceiling and started to cry. The lamp broke, she said. I've been stuck up there for half an hour, looking for it, and like a boor you didn't offer any help. People are dying and you're getting drunk. Doing nothing. The only lamp we own breaks and you just stand there. She snatched my glass away and threw it to the ground. The 'araq splashed up, white, its pungent smell spreading between the shattered glass. There was glass on my clothes. My wife came up to me and threw me out of the kitchen. Go on, get lost. I went to the balcony and sat alone. During the night, in the shelter, and amid everyone's breathing, my wife lay beside me and breathed regularly. Then she began to sob. Crying, she moved over toward me, and I moved over toward her. When we'd finished, she told me I smelled of 'araq and that she didn't like that smell.

2

Everything begins at eight o'clock in the morning. The employees come in quietly, greet one another. One of them opens up a newspaper, heads cluster, peer down or move away. Then the din starts. Scores of people brandishing medical forms. Kamel Abu Mahdi tries to control the lines. Keep the order, fellows, it'll all get done in order. But no one respects the order. The rooms fill up with the smell of people coming in from everywhere. Kamel Abu Mahdi strives diligently to process the formalities quickly. He sits behind something akin to a glass window, his bald patch glistening with sweat, holding a smudged piece of kleenex which he passes over his head and face and uses to swat at the flies buzzing in the room. He puts the kleenex down, receives some medical document, records it in a big register in front of him. He's very meticulous. Checks the doctor's signature—no fraudulent form can escape the notice of Kamel Abu Mahdi. He's come to know their tricks. They come here yelling, pushing, and shoving, and when they reach his glass window, their faces take on expressions of misery and affliction. They're sick, or were sick. And to prove it, their faces lengthen and their eyes look down forlornly. On my honor, Mr. Kamel. But Mr. Kamel isn't concerned with appearances; he checks everything for himself. That's why the queue in front of his window is always slow. All the employees of the medical security department have lots of time to chat except this bald one. For he's a man of principle, that's what they say. But the bald one has his own opinion on the matter: he can't, that's what he tells his wife when he goes home in the evening, worn out. Of course, he doesn't tell his wife that he has lots of time to chat—but that's in the afternoons. This department's working hours are quite special; it's the only government department that works in the afternoons. In the morning, the people and the smells; and in the afternoon—well, some people come, but the greater part of the time is spent gossiping and reading. Kamel Abu Mahdi doesn't like gossiping. He doesn't feel he fits in. Most of the employees are still university students, whereas he hates the university. When the employees talk about the university, he puts his bald head between his hands, his dirty fingernails showing, and stares down at the table. The same as when Wafa pesters him; she's the pretty employee with whom Kamel tried to carry out his decision to be unfaithful to his wife, and who turned him down in an incredible way: she agreed. She said let's meet in one of the cafés on Hamra Street. Kamel went there, after having despaired of convincing his wife he had to visit the boss on a Sunday afternoon. He waited for three hours in the cafe, streaming with sweat for fear someone he knew should see him. Then, all of sudden, Hani appeared with the rest of the employees, all laughing. From then on, Kamel decided that being unfaithful was an even more complicated matter than the university. He looks up at Wafa talking to him with a lot of self-assurance. You're mistaken, Kamel. You should finish your geography degree. Education is better than this dump. He looks at her, not knowing what to answer. As for her, she withholds the smile which she distributes so liberally to the rest of the employees.

We were sitting around the glasses of ʿaraq and Kamel was drinking with us.

—Why don't you always drink with us Mr. Kamel?

—Boy, I don't know how you manage. You know the reason why, everyone knows. It's marriage. A wife and kids, and you expect me to succeed. Studying is over as far as I'm concerned. I must organize myself on the basis that I'm a functionary. The truth, do you want the truth? He gulps down the glass in one go. I got married because I didn't succeed. Marriage was the only way out. I don't know how it happened. Of course, I loved her in the modern way.

—But why shouldn't we get drunk together?

This Hani, he asks a lot of questions. He wants to know my life history. Look, brother, I don't like staying up late, I like to spend time with the family. Of course, I curse the TV shows, the way everyone does. But once it starts, I don't budge from my chair. I on one side and my wife on the other. She makes a running commentary, especially during the Arabic feature. She likes Abdel-Halim Hafez.* I'm easy.

All the employees have lunch at the restaurant opposite the office except Mr. Kamel. He runs out at one o'clock, looks fearfully—right, left—before crossing the street, reaches the bus and climbs on. He prefers to sit. If there's an empty seat, he looks for another one next to a woman. If he fails to find one, he contents himself with an ordinary seat. But if he does find one, he spends the entire journey clearing his throat, looking at his watch, doubting its exactitude, before finally making his move. That doesn't usually happen until he's a few minutes from home. He asks the lady what the time is and she usually turns away and doesn't answer. But he's content with the fragrance of her perfume wafting over to him. Then he goes back to the office at three o'clock, running, the way he left.

Everything used to go smoothly. Even surprises occurred in an orderly fashion before this war. My dreams were comprehensible. As for now, everything's changed, and even football images have faded from my mind. Of course, I like football, everyone likes football. Who can forget Mardeek? Mardeek, who kept the ball between his feet, playing around with it while the other players just looked on because they couldn't do anything else. Mardeek fired up, Mardeek firing people up. We didn't forget Mar-

---

* An Egyptian singer and popular film star throughout the Arab world where he is still something of an idol. A young girl committed suicide when he died, prematurely, of bilharzia in 1977.

deek until TV came along. Then, everyone discovered that Mardeek was just an ordinary player. And I'm the only one left on this planet who's still faithful to Mardeek. My wife brought me my morning cup of coffee. She woke me as usual. I got up as usual. And, as usual, I sat at the table and ate, then drank my coffee.

What's this paunch, my wife said. Now, Kamel, you really should . . .

I didn't let her go on. I was elsewhere. Of course, I didn't tell her why I'd gotten up. I didn't tell her that the football pitch was green, like the American University field. Green grass up to your knees and drizzle blowing on our faces, Mardeek and I. We were face to face. He was wearing the green jersey and I the white, surrounded by players, water flying about our heads and between our feet. Mardeek took the ball between his feet and played around with it. I was running, with Mardeek, the king, in his place, the ball between his feet; it circled and he circled with it, with me running around it. My panting was audible while he just stood there, as if he wasn't playing. Then I dropped to the ground with exhaustion. The players came, the referee blew his whistle, they gave me a lemon, I bit into it; laid out on the green grass with the players all around me, Mardeek not budging from his place and the ball looming larger and larger until it became as large as a car. I stood up. We resumed the confrontation. I shouted, the applause welled up. My wife was beside me, holding a glass of milk. Then, it poured down rain.

No one in the medical security department knew anything about Kamel Abu Mahdi. No one visited him except Hani. Thus Hani was the only source of information. Everyone complained about this man's avarice and the roundness of his paunch. Doesn't drink coffee, doesn't smoke, rarely gets drunk. Low-down and mean. And Hani smiled. Of course, he's mean. But he works hard. He laughed and we laughed.

Kamel Abu Mahdi comes in smiling and sits behind the glass. He smiles at everyone and doesn't check the papers meticulously. He laughs, winks at Wafa. Nobody understands. Even Hani didn't know why when the employees asked him. At one o'clock, after the smell of people disperses, Kamel doesn't run for the bus. He dawdles. I'm going home. He stands up. Then goes toward his only friend. They link arms and go out together. Everybody waits. It was white and second-hand and it resembled a beetle. Volkswagen was its name. But it was a car. My wife's opinion is quite definite. She gazes at it from the balcony on the fourth floor: look, it's long, not the way you described it. It really is elongated, from the fourth floor. But it looks like a box, they all said. I know they envy me. And I envy my wife. She's completely rejuvenated. She looks like the young girls now. But I don't know where she got it from. How she collected the cash left over from my miserable salary, negotiated with the seller and bought it, how she persuaded me that the debts don't matter. I've forgiven her everything. The cups of coffee I haven't had, the restaurants I haven't been to, the friends I haven't made, everything. I've become a real man. Beirut is like a whore, you can't deal with a whore unless your pockets are full. And you can't roam around Beirut unless you're riding. Otherwise, they ride you roughshod, demean you. I'm a responsible man, and I own a car. That's why I must deal with the car responsibly.

The car's in the streets of the city. The motor behind, the steering easy, and everything is very good. I look joyfully at my wife. This woman has a special flavor now. I've become a successful employee. I'm no longer afraid. Now everybody wants to be my friend. Everybody loves the car. But my wife lays down the rules. The car is for work. Only on Sundays, we go to Rawsheh and cruise along slowly. The car's like a person. It can die. This car must not die.

The most important thing is how car lights shine on people. Car lights are amazing things. Under their beam, people glisten as if you'd put them in a pool of water. But for the neon. The neon lights erected on every street ruin the pleasure. And my wife doesn't like the village where the roads are dark and a car's a car. I don't know why I've begun to think that my wife looks like the car. When I told her that, her face shook she was so upset. But the car's more beautiful. True, it'll become decrepit, but it'll be from the inside, whereas people disintegrate from both within and without. From that day on, my wife stopped moralizing. The power to stop a woman moralizing is equivalent to getting to the moon. But the car's something special. I now go wherever I want and I've discovered the truth about these people. I used to be afraid of them. I was a new employee, I'd been transferred here from the Ministry of Public Works after a conflict with the boss that almost drove me mad. A boss is something unimaginable, something trashy to be precise. Trashier than the trashiest of employees. Like flies: you swat them but they keep coming back to sit on your neck until you give up in disgust. When I came here, I decided not to interfere in anything. Just to work and keep my head down. But then I discovered that the problem isn't the boss, it's the employees. A right proper gang they were, and they needed a victim. I was the victim. And for the first time ever, I was struck by real fear, became like a fly and started to hate my bald patch. They've finally been exposed. They're all rats. And where have they got to? They're just like me. I, at least, put my life on the line without going too far. But they're like me and I'm like them and glory be to the car. I knew that they didn't need a ride but wanted something else. They wanted to laugh at me, but openly this time. They laughed a lot but when I started to laugh the game fell apart, and so did the family. The world is extremely complicated, I'd tell her. But she didn't understand why I stayed out late and came back smelling of 'araq. I never brought 'araq into the house until this war. What else is there to do, brother, but get drunk and read the papers? Even Hani, I thought, was like the rest of them. But he died. Death transforms things. You don't understand someone until they die. And the others, my friend, they didn't die. And I didn't die. So then, we're rats.

The car rolled along. Ahmed was screaming in the back with the others, we were going to have dinner in Rawsheh. I wasn't carrying any money but they were. The roads were wet with the autumn rain. The ground was slippery as soap. Be careful, I was careful. But the ground was like one huge bar of soap. The car slid along slowly. The car was like soap. Small, like bath-soap and with a smell all its own. They were laughing and I wasn't careful. Then things began to go round. I didn't understand why things were going round until I saw the blood on my face. Everybody was shouting, it's all right. I was seeing soap everywhere. It was white and it covered everything. Like in films where the beautiful heroine is in the bath and the soap covers everything and we think we're seeing it all. The blood trickled down to my hand, my hand took on the shape of a multi-fragrant bar of soap. Really, it wasn't serious, that's what we said as we sat in the restaurant, drinking 'araq and laughing. My teeth hurt. I tried to remember exactly what had happened. The car skidded, you lost control of the steering, then your face fell on it as the car went round and round. It's nothing at all. My teeth are hurting, I told them. Soak them in 'araq, it's the best remedy. We ate and drank. Then Ahmed Ayyash stood up. He took the 'araq bottle and swallowed it neat. Then he started up. Our land in the South . . . everyone roared with laughter. Ahmed sat down and told the story. He always whispers it in my ear when he's drunk. Everyone interrupted, laughing. Acre . . . to-bacco leaves in the sun. My father died—he used to tell me about the tobacco leaves. Then they told him the land wasn't his. He was sure he'd inherited it from his father. But as to how and why . . . The title deed, they told him. The title deed means that the land is registered in the name of an-other man who owns all the land in the area.* My father almost went mad. He had to give half the harvest to a man he didn't know, who'd never set foot in the village. Ahmed Ayyash bowed his head and snored. We thought: he's asleep. But he was imitating the gestures of the stranger who'd come to the village, beaten his father and thrown him into prison. When Father came out, he died of cancer. Brother, what idiocy is this. An idiotic nation visited with djinns and rules and regulations. Ahmed waved his hand through the air. He seized the bottle of 'araq and threw it to the ground. The waiter came, had harsh words with him.

The nicest thing in the restaurant is the men's room. It's nicer than the table all laid out with food. It's undoubt-edly part of modern civilization. We went to the men's room, Ahmed and I. We stood side by side in front of the urinals. Ahmed was on the point of vomiting. But he said he could control himself. Then, after we'd finished, Ahmed took a quarter from his pocket and put it in the plate. In modern men's rooms, there's always a plate, a bottle of cheap cologne, an old woman, and a chair. Most of the time,

---

* This seemingly senseless statement is the author's ironical portrayal of what happened in Palestine, where landowners with a title to their land under Ottoman law were often dispossessed by the Zionists who "proved" to them by a variety of means that they had no such title.

the old woman leaves the chair empty and goes off. It's up to the customers to understand and put money in the plate. That night, the woman was there. She was staring at the ceiling, holding a handkerchief. Ahmed put the quarter in the plate then put his arm round my shoulder. He thought he was whispering and I was sure he was. But the old woman stood up, her eyes filled with terror. Her face was strange. Full of wrinkles with long hair straggling from her chin. But Ahmed insisted she was pretty. Maybe so, I said. But she's old and she won't accept.

—They all accept. You don't understand a thing. I'm an expert on women. You're married and sexually hung up.

—Let's try.

—Let's.

He approached her. The woman turned on her heels. The floor was orange and the woman was orange. Ahmed advanced slowly, lurching. The woman raised her hand as if to stop something.

—Sons of bitches. At my age, they want to turn me into a whore for 25 piastres.

The woman's hair was long and it hung matted about her shoulders, very fuzzy and reddish. Ahmed stepped forward. I stepped forward. The woman stepped back, she was against the wall. A sound like a lament welled up. Then she disappeared. I don't know how she disappeared, as if the earth'd split open and swallowed her up. She disappeared with the plate of money and the bottle of cologne and the chair. Ahmed cursed, I cursed. Then we went back to our seats to find that everyone wanted to go.

The car was pulling to one side. They were all afraid, I wasn't. The car isn't frightening. They stopped me. They sat on the pavement; I sat beside them, then they threw up. I tried but I couldn't. I stuck my finger down my throat, but I couldn't. Then they all left. They said I was drunk and that they were afraid and the best thing was to take a taxi. Naturally, I refused. How could I leave the car. When they'd gone, I felt really frightened. I'm drunk. I must not drive. I got off the pavement and started to push it, holding it by the door with my hand on the steering wheel. Half of me was outside the car and half of me inside. And the wheel kept slipping from my grip as though it had turned into soap. Then I got home, I don't know how. I don't know what my wife said but I remember she made sure the car was there on the street in front of the building.

Kamel Abu Mahdi was sitting by himself on a wicker chair on the balcony of the fourth floor. He jumped when he heard the voice. He grabbed the empty *'araq* bottles and ran. The lift was out of order, so he took to the stairs four by four. Then fell. The bottles shattered into shards and blood started trickling down his hand. Kamel Abu Mahdi went back, washed and bandaged his hands, then sat down again on the balcony. The old man had aged, he was more stooped and the cart in front of him was practically a wreck. The voice was faint: scrap metal for sale, glass bottles for sale. Next to him was a small boy all proud of himself. Holding the bottles up, knocking them against each other musically. People buying and selling.

3

It was pouring rain. I came home from work exhausted and stopped the car on the street below the balcony. But I didn't find a place. I tried to park the car in its usual place and finally succeeded. I went up to the house, I was hungry. The four children were leaping about the house, screeching. I washed my face, told my wife I was hungry. But eating has its own rites. The children must go to bed first. I sat and waited for the children in the living-room. The radio was making ugly noises. I think I fell asleep. Then when I opened my eyes, Ahmed Ayyash and Hani and Zuheir were standing there, towering above me. I was hungry. My wife told me there was rice and *fasoolia*.* Ahmed Ayyash sucked in his breath as if you were inviting him to make love to a woman. But *fasoolia* doesn't mean a thing with 'araq. He darted out and came back a second later with a bottle of 'araq in his hand. We sat at the table and drank, taking our time. We mustn't get drunk, said Mr. Zuheir, humorless as a shoe. We drank and talked shop. The same dumb talk, of the boss, of this and that. Naturally, we didn't talk about women out of due respect for my wife; then they began to talk about things that reminded me of university and of the honorable sheikh—may he rest in peace—who'd put his turban down and lecture on the greatness of Omar Bin Khattab.**

Everything's changing. We're a nation without civilization. And Ahmed Ayyash went off into his religious trance. The conversation got sticky, like the beans between our teeth. Our lips and the rims of our 'araq glasses were smudged red. The plates in front of us and next to the plates, the forks that no one used. Hands reaching out to pieces of bread. You mix the white beans swimming in the red with the white rice then put them in your mouth after swilling it with a bit of 'araq. Everything in this conversation was becoming repetitive like cooking. Mr. Zuheir was clearing his throat, he wanted to speak.

—Cheers.

We drank to our health.

---

* A *yakhneh* (see note on p. 101) of dried white beans. It is hearty, ordinary people's food, not a refined dish.

** The second caliph who ruled between 632 A.D. and 644 A.D. Under him, Islam witnessed its first great expansion from Arabia to the Fertile Crescent, Egypt and Iran. He is thus a potent symbol of all that is best in Islam and a source of pride for those who yearn for a renewal in the Arab world.

Everything's changed, Mr. Zuheir said.

Everything's changed, we answered him.

—No, it's true. But there's one thing that hasn't changed or been replaced. *Yakhneh*.* *Yakhneh* is the essence of civilization. The Turks are a civilized people. Forget language and the rest. They subjugated us with their cooking. Stuffed courgettes is a good dish. You bet it's good. But it needs a Turkhead to make it.

Our civilization is alive and well. Long live our civilization. We drank to our undying civilization. Then the food and the conversation finished and we started to yawn.

The rain was torrential. Naturally, they said to Kamel there's no need and, naturally, he insisted. They went down together. He drove them home and came back alone in his car. He drove slowly through the rain. He felt slightly cold. But driving was a pleasure. And Kamel loves his pleasures.

When I got home, I was in a fix. Someone had taken my parking place . . . so I had to park the car far from the house. I bolted down the street, getting soaked, and went in. My wife was in bed. I took off my clothes, put on my pajamas and slipped in next to her. I was cold. This central heating of ours doesn't work properly. Landlords are all meaner than dogs. They bleed us white in the name of modern buildings, then switch off the central heating before the pipes have even heated up. I was sure she was faking sleep. I stretched my hand out to her. Her body was hot. I moved closer, her smell filled the air. She wasn't my wife, she was a woman. 'Araq can do anything. I kissed her and climbed on to her body like a young man seeing a woman for the first time. And she moved closer, then away a little, holding me. I plunged into her. The nicest thing in the world is a woman who laughs as you make love to her. I was

* Originally a Turkish word used in much of the Levant to mean stew.

hard and leaned over her as she swayed in my arms, swooning.

—We don't want any children, she whispered, laughing.

—You're nicer than children.

She bowed her head. You're making fun of me. I wasn't making fun of her. I was taking her into my arms and swaying. Children are born and cry. Their faces are grubby and their feet muddy. She was beautiful.

I don't know how I fell asleep but she woke me up. I'm scared, she said. That's her old trick. A woman's a woman. Whenever I sleep with her and fall asleep, she wakes me up because she wants more. And I always submit to her desire. But not today. I'm tired, I've drunk a lot, no way. I pretended to be fast asleep. I turned my back to her and snored my usual way. But she insisted. I felt her hand on my back, trembling.

—I'm scared.

I sat up and pretended to be startled like any man waking up from sleep.

—The noise, don't you hear the noise.

—It's the rain. I want to sleep. Understood?

I got up. She followed me. No doubt an open window in the living-room. The window was open and the rain all over the carpet. I closed the window. My wife rolled up the carpet and swept the living-room. I felt her seducing me. She swept in a bizarre way. No. It was the see-through nightie. We went to bed. I want to sleep, I told her. She took my hand. I lit a cigarette. She fell asleep as the cigarette glowed in the room.

I wept. The corpse was in front of me, with people all around it, but the corpse was before me alone. Kamel Abu Mahdi stood dazed. His bald head trembled, his hand tried to brush something off his forehead. I don't know where the women came from. Women on the pavements, holding handkerchiefs, laughing.

I told my wife that the car.

I told the woman standing in front of me that the car. But she pointed to a little girl running in the street and laughed.

I told her that . . .

She said that the shells.

Kamel Abu Mahdi stood alone. It was all alone in front of me. The street was full of shrapnel shards; the street was full of glass; the street was full of cars. But it had died. He went toward it. The front tire blew out. The rubber resembled chewing-gum. The street was full of black rubber that looked like soldiers' boots. I told them we should move the car. The black rubber was spreading. I gripped the tires. Kamel Abu Mahdi kneeled. Everyone watached. He was gripping the rubber, trying to move it. He stood up, wiped his face. It was black. He knew he shouldn't cry. It can't be true, he said to his wife. The tears fell nevertheless. Tears are like nothing else. He sat down on the pavement, his head in his hands, and it rained.

They said to him: shame on you, really, Mr. Kamel.

He said to them: shame, but she died.

They said to him that the shell.

He said, never mind.

He stood up. There was glass on his lips. The steering wheel was broken in two. He went over to the engine: metal devouring metal. It looked like what you saw in pictures. He touched it. Her skin was dry and blisters covered his hands. He held her, he told her. She didn't answer. He told his wife, his wife didn't answer.

The wife said that the war.

I said to her. The war.

But the war. Fish are prettier. The shell wouldn't fall anywhere but on my head.

Sameer stepped forward, rifle in hand, never mind, Sameer said.

Never mind, Mr. Kamel said. Everything's never mind.

Never mind death, the wife said.

They were laughing. Imm Jameel stood there, holding her new baby girl. Never mind, neighbor. God be praised, you're safe. No one was injured. Money comes and money goes.

But it goes. Ever since I've known it, it's been going. It's never once come. It only ever goes.

Imm Jameel was making fun of us. Her husband owns a car. Honestly, you're an idiot, my wife said. Why did you park the car there?

I told my wife I was an idiot. But the shell, that's what the shell wanted. I told her the car had died. This woman abhors me. She despises me. I'm sure of it.

—Why did you park the care there?

—I parked it in its place.

—But the shelling.

I sat on the chair, all by myself. Picked up the newspaper and tried to read. My wife was standing in front of me, crying. I didn't say anything. The city was shaking. Even the street was no longer tenable. The small cars standing in a long line, one behind the other, as though awaiting execution.

They told Kamel, it won't do. The smell. The smell of rubber and the disgusting sight of it. He wouldn't listen. No way. I'm going to try to repair it. He told his wife the insurance company had to pay. She laughed. Sameer told Kamel the car had to be towed away. The smell, the children, you know. Kamel was desperate. I beg you. He wouldn't hear of it. He told them all right. The tow-truck came. They slung the cables down and tied them to the car. They dragged it through the streets, the sound of the metal grating against the asphalt was painful . . . they were flaying it. He followed behind. The tow-truck proceeded slowly, young men shouting, children watching, the wife on the balcony. And Kamel walked behind his car. He told them. But it went.

I'm the only one who hasn't stopped going to work. I now go to the office on foot. I sit by myself. I answer the boss's phone calls. I listen to his opinions and to his advice. Everything's changed. Even the boss's voice has greatly changed. It's become gentle. He tells jokes and asks after the family. And at the end of the month everyone turns up to get his pay. Why don't I do the same? I'm the only civil servant left in the Lebanese Republic. But I can't. What would I do at home? There's no one there but the neighborhood youths, with their weapons, laughing and dying. Even my wife has changed—she says it's because of the war. She can't take the war anymore. I'm sure she's changed since the car died. She despises me. My father always said women were fearsome: one lapse and they lord it over you. You have to keep your ground before her. Everything lapses: the car, the job and . . . And me, on my own, with the newspapers, the 'araq and my black thoughts.

Then the office came to a standstill. It would open only at the end of each month, pay-day. . . . There were shells now everywhere, everyone slept in shelters. And Kamel argued with his wife and the children bawled. He would go down to the street, mingling with the lads, getting to know them. He'd feel their rifles, was impressed with such courage that doesn't fear death. He'd ask for news of the fighting. They'd tell him. Of course, they'd lie a little.

But the sound of the explosions proved to him that there was a real war going on. And that these lads were fighting a war just like the ones we read about in books. The sight of the confiscated loot dazzled him—the colored shirts, the new clothes. He refused a shirt offered him as a gift but then accepted it the following day.

His wife wailed: unlawful wealth. Everything's unlawful, he answered her, and went back down to the street. But best of all were the cars. Every day a newly requisitioned car. Kamel toyed with the idea of driving the new car.

—I'll drive you guys.

—But we're going to Wadi Abu Jameel. There's sniping on the way.

—I'm a good driver. Don't worry. He got into the car, turned on the ignition. Then turned it off . . . I'm busy now. Never mind, I'll drive you over tomorrow. They laughed. He smiled at them. He'd made up his mind to decide on the thing he'd been dreaming of for a long time and didn't dare announce: I must go with them. There, I'll find cars. But how to go? My wife's gone mad and the tire still stares me in the face. I must get rid of the tire first. The tire was in the house, in the bedroom. Kamel had bought a new tire for his car even though all four of its tires were fine. A spare, he told his wife; he didn't tell her that he had bought it because it was going cheap.

—We should put it in the trunk.

But she wouldn't hear of it.

—The trunk's too small and it's for the stroller and bits and pieces. She convinced me. We put the tire in the room. Then the car died. I want to throw it away. But she won't allow it.

—We'll take out the inner tube and the children'll use it to swim at the beach.

She's ridiculing me. She despises me. Kamel Abu Mahdi grabbed the tire, picked it up, went out of door, and rolled it down the stairs. The tire was going down the stairs, Kamel following behind, with eyes and body. The man screamed. The tire had hit him. Men haven't got much of a sense of humor these days. He cursed, I cursed back. He drew his pistol. Holding it in his right hand, he came toward me. I didn't know this man. He came toward me. The tire lay there like a corpse. He advanced, put his pistol up to my face, and begun punching my jaw with his left fist. I didn't feel any pain, but shook before the gun-barrel. The man went on up. I followed behind, entered the house, didn't breathe a word.

4

The confiscations are something else. What a city — a whore of a city. Who can imagine a whore laying a million men and still being there. A city with a million shells falling on it and still there. The city *is* shells. And thirst. A city without water. Never mind the electricity, we can always buy another lamp. But water . . . Even the sweat on our bodies has become just salt. There isn't any water left to sweat and dirty the shirts with. The city is salty. I couldn't take it anymore. Sameer gave me his pistol. He told me he'd come with me, but he never did. I was scared. There were no more policemen and I was still scared. I stuck the pistol on my hip, the way everyone does, and waited on the street. But Sameer didn't come. I was scared — Beirut is long in the darkness and the noise of the shells. The man was walking through the darkness alone. He lit a match which cast his shadow against the walls of the half-deserted city. Then the match went out and the shadow with it. The noise faraway was getting closer, and the man was walking practically bent in two, hugging the wall. In the streets, the cats were yawning. And the smell welled up alongside the mounds of garbage. The man who walked hugging the wall was trying to find his way through these things. He got closer. It was as though the parked cars were asleep. He went on, then came to a stop in front of a Volkswagen. He lit a match, but it was ugly. The pistol on his hip trembled. He reached the Zokak al-Blatt intersection where you cut across the wide street and reach the entrance of Wadi Abu Jameel with its abandoned cars and destroyed houses. And the war. Beirut, completely still, immersed in darkness. Then the sounds of light sniper-fire began. He felt the street reeling with every shot. Then the heavy machine-gun rang out. He stepped back. Everything was shaking. He decided to go back. He turned his back to the wide street and set off slowly. He felt a gun-barrel was aimed at his back. His neck was heavy now, as though the barrel were up against it. He went a little faster, the sound of his footsteps merging into the gunfire. He was panting and it was still a long way home. Rats springing between his feet and salt spreading over his entire body.

By the time Kamel got home, he was convinced of it. The car had died. But my wife was shrieking. I acted serious. I wanted to mislead her into thinking that I was with the lads. She yelled at me as if I were a little kid. She looked like a goat, letting off the sort of noises a hungry goat does. She marched me to the shelter. I told her I wanted to sleep in my own bed. She refused, she took me to the shelter, and I slept next to her.

Apart from children and vegetable sellers, everyone's afraid of artillery shells. It used to be that there was shelling at night and the daytime was for the children. But even this law they desecrated: now there was shelling day and night. The women pretended not to notice and the children were out on the street. Shells flying. A car bursting into flames inside the garage. Where are the children, shrieked my wife.

She ran, I followed behind. The street was all torn up and the children were crowding about. My wife wailed. All women wail. I saw the color red. I looked: my wife was standing in front of the children in the building lobby. I yelled at her to go up home. Come up with us, she yelled back. Her hair was long and she was covered in blood. She was sprawled against the pavement over a pool of blood, like a pretty sheep drinking water. No one came near. All the men stood around the building entrances. Then a boy wearing glasses came along. He picked the girl up. The salt spread. The blood spilled onto his face and clothes. He carried her, put her in his orange car, and went. Then they said that she died and we took to spending the day in the shelter. When Sameer and the lads came along with the blue poster, I couldn't believe it. The poster was blue and it was the same boy. The glasses, the round face. The red writing. Talal, they said his name was. I looked at the poster, blood spilling onto the glossy blue paper, over the white print and the slogans. The blood of the girl who looked like a sheep covered the walls of the city. I remembered Hani and cried. The boy looked out from the poster as if from a window. His eyes motionless, the blood trickling over them. But they're like my mother's eyes, I told him. The girl was salty. Even the color of blood isn't important, it's just salty and hot. Everything that has a taste has a smell, except salt. Salt hasn't got a smell but it floods one's mouth. It grows on one's hands and shoulders and spreads into the hair on one's head. The poster, beside the other posters, covering the walls and bleeding like a sheep to a mounting rhythm in the undestroyed city.

I was thirsty. She said, there's no water. I went a

long way, all the way to the public garden filled with flies. I washed my face. Filled the containers. But the salt clung to my clothes.

Kamel Abu Mahdi no longer understands. He's taken to saying the newspapers are colorless, but he reads like everybody else, listens to the radio like everybody else and believes in God like everybody else. Beirut was sparkling like a ship with its lights turned off in the middle of the dark sea. Everybody sleeping. In a deathlike stillness — the stillness of ceasefires — when suddenly the city was ablaze with light. All the houses lit up together amid bursting gunfire and joy. Everybody woke up and celebrated. Beirut had come home. Kamel Abu Mahdi awoke, sat out on the balcony leaving all the house lights on. And with the electricity, water returned. His wife got up and filled every container in the house. Electricity and water, the essence of happiness, thought Kamel. When he said as much to his wife, she cursed him. Get up and help me carry the water. But he didn't get up. He was going to enjoy the electricity to the last. He wanted to breathe in the smell of Beirut which they said had died. He had a cup of coffee and stayed up till three in the morning when the electricity was cut off. He went back to bed happy. But he dreamed the car had come home. It was covered in dust and mud. It came back alone, climbed the stairs, knocked at the door and came in. It was full of hair, it looked like a dog. It barked, rubbed its mouth against its paws, circled around him. It had no eyes. He went up to it, found it as he'd left it. He sat up front, held the steering wheel with both hands. It disintegrated and his head crashed against the window. The window broke. The seat began to sound an uninterrupted moan. Wearing the white wedding dress, a red bouquet in her hand, Kamel's wife was seated opposite him and smiling for the pictures. He wanted to tell her the car had come back and that it looked like a dog but that it had no tail. He wanted to tell her the steering wheel had broken but that it could be repaired. He wanted to tell her everything but she never turned toward him. She was looking at the photographer and smiling. Kamel was pouring with sweat. He opened the car door. It wouldn't open. His wife was turning red, the color of the girl who died. The woman was opening her mouth to say something, blood streamed out of her mouth and nose. Kamel stuck his head out of the window and saw that the man was naked. But he had no genitals. He screamed. His voice was dry. And the walls of the house were covered in salt. Terrified, Kamel got up. Found nothing. Wife asleep, kids asleep, the whole city asleep. So he went back to bed.

But the war didn't come to an end. All those who said that the war had ended knew this war wouldn't end. Darkness returned to the city along with the sound of the shells. War comes back all of a sudden. It comes to a halt slowly, after long negotiations and interventions and prominent figures and the radio and the favorite newscaster all the employees like because he's an employee like them. But it comes back all of a sudden. The electricity goes off, the shelling starts and people rush to corridors and shelters, to the safe rooms and to the houses overlaid by houses.

I don't know how I woke up. The building was shaking. Smoke and voices. My wife screamed. I screamed. The kids everywhere. We ran. The ground gleamed. We stood in the corridor next to the kitchen. The children were crying. My wife said let's go down to the shelter. She ran, flung the door open. We went down. The crush of people. The whole world's tenants on the building stairs, rushing for the shelter. I carried my little daughter. The two boys were in front of me and my wife was holding the bawling, half-naked baby. I didn't ask her why the child was half-naked. They all looked like ghosts, running with their matches and candles. The women in nighties and the men barefoot, and the children falling over and picking themselves up. Dust and smoke. I started coughing. My wife clutching my sleeve. The two boys clutching her legs and I clutching the wall. The wall was shaking, moaning, smoking. I tried to go faster—but the crush of people, what can you do. Everybody screaming. You, he shouted. I said to myself I don't know, it's not anything to do with me, I'm just an ordinary citizen. He was standing on the stairs in front of me.

—Why did you throw the tire down?

I told him it fell. He raised his pistol. It glimmered. He held it with both hands, a terrifying noise came out. Never mind, I told him. He advanced, placed the pistol between my eyes. I could no longer see. He hit me with his left fist. I fell to the ground. Got up. He hit me again and I fell once more. My mouth was bleeding. I'll bash your head in. I didn't look up. I went back to the house and didn't tell my wife I was scared.

I'm scared, she yelled. I didn't answer. These stairs are so long, I told her. And it was dark. Everyone had vanished.

—Where's the box of matches?

—I forgot it. I'll go up and get it.

—Don't leave me alone, I'm scared.

I told her, I'm scared, where have they gone? There wasn't a soul left. My wife clutched my sleeve and the children were crying.

—I forgot the baby's bottle at home.

I didn't say I'd go and get it. The baby fell from my wife's arms and cried. I didn't hear her crying. The blood. The shells getting closer. The smoke creeping up on us. And the thick darkness. My wife screamed and then began to sob. We went on down. Silence and smoke. The shelling had stopped. But the smoke. In the dark, you can't see anything but smoke. We went slowly down, the steps quite firm. Interminable stairs.

They were six living things, going down the stairs slowly. Darkness enveloping the stairway and smoke enveloping the darkness. The woman crying silently. Interminable stairs. Kamel Abu Mahdi knows these stairs well. Eighty of them. He counts them going up and counts them again going down. But he's forgotten to count with this shelling. We've surely gone beyond that. He can taste salt all of a sudden. There's salt on my lips, he told his wife. Where did the salt come from. I said to her there's salt in my clothes. I heard her moan. Going down very slowly, descending these interminable stairs. I leaned against the wall. It was salty and making sounds like those of distant trains. Down, down slowly. My wife next to me, the kids between our legs and the stairs slow. Where's the water, I signaled with my hand. No one saw me. I went on down the stairs very slowly.

Chapter 5

The KING'S SQUARE

I was walking in my sodden clothes through the damp passages with their moldy smell of rain, looking for the way in the unfamiliar tunnels, cursing and trying not to look ridiculous. Ever since I arrived in this city, I've been going from hospital to hospital, from doctor to doctor and all of them—doctors and nurses all—shake their heads. They carry out tests and say: nothing, we don't know, maybe tomorrow. Results and yet more results till I'm just about overcome by hysteria and anxiety. Since last night, and after a long day of suffering and interrogation, I've decided to be very careful: I must not appear ridiculous. I realized this the first time a nurse took hold of my hand. Stretched out on a plastic mat, my arm had thousands of sharp needles stuck into it. There were three nurses around me. A nurse smiled then began to sew my hand down to the plastic mat. Trying to distract me, she asked what I did for a living. I told her I didn't do anything. The second nurse drew near and said: do you know how much you're going to have to pay for this medical examination?

—No, I don't.
—Three hundred and eighty-five francs.
—I won't pay.

—We'll put you in jail.

Here, I burst out laughing. The air was charged with something or other so the laughter exploded and the nurses laughed too.

—Buy why are you laughing?

—Because prisons are temporary things, I told her. We've abolished prisons. We were even about to abolish hospitals but for some rather complicated considerations. There wasn't really the time to tell her how the children in our neighborhood once overran the women's prison and carried off its rooftop—they dismounted the terra-cotta tiles one by one. The atmosphere just wasn't conducive. Anyway, the important thing then was my arm. Of course, I paid up the entire amount afterward, though not for fear of imprisonment or the nurse, but just like that, because I felt sad. The electric current rushed through my left arm. I groaned, the nerve throbbed fiercely, on and on. Take a deep breath, scream, the nurse instructed. I breathed but my face was all twisted. It is then that I discovered the smiles on the nurses' faces. Contorted in an ocean of pain, my own face no doubt looked funny. I tried to control my nerves and stop the muscles contracting. I stopped breathing but I couldn't. The pain flooded my body, the electricity annihilating it. Then suddenly, everything stopped. I got up from the chair and walked, tried walking quickly and fell down. Don't forget you're sick, the nurse said. She smiled when I paid up the entire amount for the examination.

I abandoned my dash through that roaring jungle. I must find the way: she's waiting for me and won't wait very long. Last time, I arrived half an hour early and I sat in a cafe and the hubbub of thousands of voices. But she never came. When I called her in the evening, she answered apologetically. We agreed to meet today but she was threatening: don't be late, I won't wait more than five minutes. So here I am trying not to be late. The problem, though, is that I can't find my way through this maze. I'm sick, these metro tunnels are complicated and half the signs have been removed. I walked calmly and stopped in front of the newspaper seller, then felt an acrid smell of wine stealing up on me. He started to embrace me, shouting: how did you get here? When did you come? I looked at him closely and had to laugh. It was Bergis Nohra, none other.

—Tell me, come on, why don't you come and visit me?

It was Bergis Nohra, none other.

—I wasn't, I don't want, I'm in a hurry, tomorrow.

But Bergis Nohra held me fast. Pulling me by the arm, come on. A stockily built man, fair-haired, thick-necked, a little prone to stoutness, talking about twenty different things at once. He was just the same five years ago. Bergis Nohra still yearns for his village. I'm a Maronite, from Bdadoun. He was just the same five years ago. I was penniless, poorer than the poorest of students. Maybe that's what made me accept his invitation. I went into a house. At last, to enter a house and sit at a real meal. I was starving and ate as if I'd never before seen food in my life. I drank, he drank; we were drinking from twelve noon until the evening. To start with, I didn't talk. It was hard making conversation as I wanted to be free to eat. After we'd got drunk and I'd been listening for a long time as he reminisced about his village and his father's bankruptcy and his adventures, he started talking politics. Spare me, I told him. But he insisted. He started talking about the *fedayeen* and the September massacres.* He spoke in a skillfully mastered military lingo.

—But how do you know all this?

—I'm a fighter. I was a real fighter, he answered.

---

* A reference to the culmination of two years of intermittent clashes, from 1968 to 1970, between the Jordanian army and the PLO in Jordan, when thousands of civilians were killed.

Of course I didn't buy his story. The small, over-hanging pot-belly and the luxurious restaurant he owns belie his claims.

—But where?

—In Vietnam.

Again, I didn't buy it. I let him talk and gave myself up to the drops of cognac. He rambled on and I wasn't lis-tening, until all hell broke loose and his voice began thun-dering through the room like a cannon. I jumped up.

—What are you saying? The Foreign Legion!

—Yes, the Foreign Legion.

—You mercenary, you less-than-nothing, you savage, you . . .

I stood up, took the bottle of cognac and hurled myself at him. He dodged. Listen, you're drunk, he shouted. You shouldn't let wine stop you treating people properly. Listen to me, I'm on your side, and on theirs, but listen. I couldn't. He ran to the bedroom and locked him-self in. I must have looked terrifying. So let me listen. I calmed down, sat on the sofa, and waited for him. He came back.

—Listen, brother, listen carefully. It's a compli-cated question. I was down and out, I didn't have a resi-dence permit in Paris. The police arrested me and gave me a choice of prison or the Foreign Legion. What would you have had me choose?

—To go back to Lebanon.

—That wasn't possible. Lebanon wasn't in the cards then. Prison or Vietnam, so I went to Vietnam. We fought a great deal but that isn't the point. The point is that we knew our defeat to be inevitable. Yet we stayed on to fight. We'd committed ourselves to the war and we were going to honor our commitment. I'm a stubborn Maronite, I don't pull out. I knew that the Foreign Legion and all the French army units would be defeated. Yet, I stayed on with them and fought because I'm a stubborn man. Then he began to laugh. Don't believe this stubborn-man story, I'm only telling it because I've drunk a lot. I tried to escape several times or, rather, to be honest with you, I thought of escaping. But it wasn't possible. War is a meticulously organized thing and the only way out of it is to stay with it. Aside from the fact that I fell in love with a Vietnamese woman and married her. Honestly, I'm not lying. I would go back to the mud hut in the evening and find her there waiting for me with the barrel. She'd put me inside and water would start to flow over me. I'd climb out, practically naked, gobble down my food with some rice wine, then gradually get drunk and just sit there. And I'd sleep with her sitting up, because standing or lying down are out of the question for anyone who drinks that wine. She was a beautiful woman. She stayed beautiful to her dying day. I believe she died when the French artillery was "combing" the Vietminh areas before the defeat at Dhien Bien Phu. Defeat was inevitable, despite my wife's death and that of thousands of others. Though they carried the cannons on bicycles and climbed up the mountains strapping them to their shoulders, surrender was unavoidable. But best of all was the barrel. My relationship to the war was two-sided: a relationship with a beautiful woman on the one hand and with a barrel, on the other.

This conversation took place five years ago and though I don't remember much, that's when Borgis Nohra became my friend. As far as I'm concerned, friendship is something quite specific, it means we get drunk once a month. For him, it was an opportunity to oust his French wife from the house and to speak Arabic. Still, when I came over this year I didn't want to see him. The civil war hasn't left a relationship unscarred and the news that the *feda-*

yeen had entered Bdadoun on one of those war nights had surely reached him. That's why I didn't want to see him. But there he was, standing in front of me, the personification of strange coincidence.

—Why don't you come and visit me. Come over right now. I want to hear your news and news of the war in Lebanon. Impossible to convince him otherwise. I'm busy now, my good Bergis. Let's get together tomorrow. As you wish. We'll talk about everything. Just when he seemed to have yielded, he started up again, as though delirious.

—Look at the metro. Look at these tunnels. What it means is that civil war is inevitable. A civil war in the passages and tunnels of the metro, it'd be mythical. Every expectation would be confounded and the earth would revert to its entrails. Something amazing!

—Even when you come to visit me, you've got to come with me to the metro. I know you've seen it. But look, look! The city penetrated by metro tunnels is shaking, it is going to cave in. Civil war here is inevitable. I've been on the metro a great deal and have visited a lot of cities but I've never uncovered the relationship between metros and tunnels and between tunnels and civil war. Cities, all cities, are alike: Some traversed by a metro, others not. But all that has nothing to do with war. In Cairo, there's a metro but it's above ground. People dart back and forth between the metro cars, the buses, and the narrow alleys. They burn tires or stop burning them. In Beirut, there's no metro and there are no tunnels. In Milan, demonstrators overturned the metro cars and the police had to close off the subway entrances to prevent people from joining the demonstrations. In Damascus, there are no such things as metro tunnels but Qassioun* is being dug up and destroyed so that they can turn it into pretty—or ugly—villas. That is the point. Cities above ground and cities under ground. After

---

* A famous hill on the edge of Damascus.

Ottoman Beirut was destroyed, they started looking for Roman Beirut under the rubble. In a nutshell, all change is geological, like earthquakes, like volcanoes. They bore through the bowels of a city to install means of communication and means of residence. But all these means serve but one end—war and death.

There we were in the middle of the metro passages, Bergis's voice soaring and me standing still, unable to do anything. That is the point, he was telling me. The point is that this city will be destroyed in a civil war. All cities will be destroyed. I was trying to say something. The point was something else but I'd started to feel frightened and said nothing. This time, I, as well as Bergis and the sound of the metro, the metro itself, all seemed ridiculous. I wasn't able to do anything not to. True enough, I'm sick. But this man just won't stop hallucinating.

—Do you see? Civil war is inevitable. People will annihilate one another. Cities will collapse. It's inevitable and I see it as clearly as I saw the pictures of the war in Beirut.

—But Bergis . . .

—Just imagine what might happen in these endlessly ramified passages with modern destructive weapons. The civil war will be the metro war. You agree, of course you do.

I don't know why I began to agree with him. It's not that the words were convincing. Nor was it the sight of Bergis ranting on feverishly, rapturously about war. His constant turning to me and taking me by the hand lest I run away were not convincing either. The truth of the matter is that I wasn't the least bit convinced by Bergis's argument, but I began to be convinced nonetheless. A man in his forties, his clothes stinking of alcohol, standing in a cacophonous jungle. People rushing about as if they were late for some appointment and I looking at my watch for fear of being late. And this man completely indifferent. Just talking on, with his hands, with his voice, with his stocky little body, swaying to and fro, prophesying devastation. And those others, rushing about, they'll rush again but for different reasons, because life cannot go on like this. Everything'll turn topsy-turvy—guns, cannons, war. Bergis rambled on and I was trying, one last time, not to appear ridiculous. But that isn't the point.

* * *

The point was over there. A woman, glowing. I held her hand and we went to the smallest room in the world. Terra-cotta tiles, white wood, yellow curtains. And she, in the center of the room, naked, laughing. Slipping from my hands to the bed, from the bed to the floor and from the floor back into my hands. A woman, glowing. Milky white. Her two eyes small, but elongated, like the eyes of the Chinese. I was holding her by her hair and drowning in the place where the pain flowed from her shoulders. I was holding her, she was falling. But not breaking. She was folding in two, I was her third half and her voice rang like a tropical garden.

I approached her, my feet dragging on the floor, grating against the wooden floor-boards. I was swaying, cleaving, getting closer. The rubescence, and her smell, spreading across the floor. I was not saying anything but was not quiet either. The apogee of sadness. She cried, sitting at the edge of the room, holding her breasts. I went toward her, frightened. No, I wasn't frightened. I was looking for something or other, for a word. But she remained on the edge of the room. Then stood up, came toward me. I held her, she dropped to the floor and broke, and the room filled with pieces of shrapnel. I bent down to pick them up, blood began to flow and the walls were covered in mud and trees. I was going up the stairs, my foothold quite firm. I could go no farther. I held her. Lights colored the sky and her body was as a dough of constantly changing tints. She took me. My body quivered as though feverish, then I fell. And it was a very long way.

She was the point. To hold her was to hold nothing. She would run off, leaving me baffled. I would run after her. That's how she imprisoned me inside a dream that was hard to abandon. That was in the autumn, when the sky reddened with the leaves and the sweeping branches of the trees. She'd be beside me, looking for me when I was lost and losing me when I found her. Everything amazed her. The trees donning their autumn reds struck her with wonder and when she looked at the sky it was if she'd not seen a sky before. Everything that used to be familiar was new. At first, I was enthralled by this new kind of life, then it began to irk me. We can't live just like that with no reference point whatsoever. I can't live like this, scattered to the winds. Except that she insisted; she lived her life the way she lived life. I began to discover life through her and plunged into the bewitchment. Once, we were running or walking down a long street lined with red trees. She was beside me, in front of me, behind me. I held her by the hair as we walked peacefully. I tried to talk to her, it wasn't possible. Talking to this woman was hard. You always had to go over everything from the beginning as if you were getting to know her this very minute. As a result, we spoke only rarely. I stopped her in the middle of the street where the red leaves grew out of her hands.

—This is the revolution, I said. Just like this, living in the constant discovery of everything, in the nothingness of everything. That is revolution.

—Me, I don't like politics.

—And me, I'm not talking about politics. I'm talking about revolution.

—But revolution is politics. Isn't revolution politics?

—However it is always beginning in spite of politics or inside of politics. It is the thing that is constantly beginning. Like love, like death, like you. She didn't answer. Her body was transluscent. No, not a mirror. The other kind of transluscence, where you don't see yourself but see beyond things as though in a dream.

I grabbed her and threw her to the water. But she wasn't a fish, she was a woman, so she began to drown. The water flowed across her face, between her breasts. But she wasn't a fish. I held her and scaled her to the very end but the end wasn't possible. That is the point.

Everything seems like that, ambiguous and incomprehensible. In the end, however, things intersect and come together to form triangles. You can't discover things, stripped bare, just like that. They all fit into triangles and triangles are the beginnings of things—or something like beginnings. Triangles fit into circles. Every triangle, whatever its shape, whatever the size of its angles, fits inside a circle. And circles necessarily burst apart. That is how I discovered our story. I couldn't start with events. Events are ambiguous, they're distorted and not susceptible to beginnings. We started off as a triangle. That was at the university. We still nurtured a few dreams about the university and were engaged in the struggle for establishing a national institution. We hadn't yet found out that a university is just an old shoe and that the dreams we coveted would turn us into shoes, if the university wasn't destroyed. And it was, of course, along with everything else in this city, but in another context. But then many things start with this triangle.

Face one: Dr. Hanna. A man about 45 years old, tall, white hair starting to speckle his head. He'd come into class in a hurry, leave in a hurry, always as if he had an appointment to keep with something. What that thing might have been wasn't clear. He was supposed to lecture on psychology. But only rarely did he talk about this psychology of his or anything else related to the topic. He always spoke to us about his childhood, about the years of poverty when he worked in a little clothing store in Souq Sursock, about how he was a self-made man, had studied, obtained his doctorate, and joined academic ranks. I don't know why, but I never believed this business about working in Souq Sursock. I judge that he did something else. He was a waiter maybe, in some café. He looked like a waiter, his elegance was reminiscent of those who work in the Hamra Street cafés. Anyhow, that's not important. The important thing was the book. He'd come into class carrying a rectangular book which he'd wave about in the air and then carefully put away in his bag. That's where I belong, I belong with the downtrodden, that's why I carry around their thoughts, their cause. The book, so far as I can remember, was about the relationship between Marxism and Christianity or humanist Marxism or some such gibberish that was fashionable in those days. We admired this professor and his humanist Marxism and his rectangular book that was written in French which we didn't understand all that well. Even more, we admired the compassion he had for his social class and his strange insistence on twisting his right hand around as he told us about the dialectic. I'm open-minded, I'm not a dogmatic Marxist. I'm a humanist, I understand and I like to be understood, and I'm fully prepared to change my mind if someone convinces me that I'm wrong. That's what the dialectic is about, it is the key to everything. He spent three years telling us about the dialectic and our delight in the wonderful dialectic grew with every passing year. Until, one day, the police came into the university looking for the radicals who don't believe in dialogue and insist on stoning them. The dialectic ran out the back door that day and dedicated himself to psychology.

Face two: his name was Yaaqub, we all loved him. He was a student and he resembled the *fahlawi* character whom Sadeq al-Athm* drove us nuts with after the June defeat—to the extent that we came to believe that there lies some such magical figure behind every defeat. But he wasn't *fahlawi*, simply a little lazy and a *bon viveur*; he loved drinking and good food, chatting and laughing. More important, he loved his friends and we all loved him. He'd come into the cafeteria carrying Aristotle's *Metaphysics*, for Yaaqub had chosen philosophy. The book began to fall apart sitting on the cafeteria table, the cover got completely frayed. But Yaaqub never found the time to read owing to his many activities. He never missed a demonstration, he'd be right up there in front, chanting and dancing before the water hoses, getting beaten by the rifle butts. He'd go home in the evening, exhausted, barely finding the time to drink a glass of *'araq*, sing a few lines of *zajal*** and then sleep. We loved him dearly. And when we went into the *fedayeen*, he came with us and became a *feda'i*. Then, he left for Europe to study. He didn't stay with us long enough to discover the games of death. Had he stayed, he would've probably joined our friends who died and we would have forgotten the Aristotle business and remembered him gun

---

* Originally a popular term, the word *fahlawi* was used by the Syrian thinker Sadeq Jalal al-Athm in his book *Self-Criticism after the Defeat (al-naqd al-d-hati ba'd al-hazimah)* to portray the Arab personality which substitutes words for action, in other words, an unproductive personality.

** A kind of formulaic poetry which is typical of the oral traditions of Syria, Lebanon, and Palestine.

in hand, keeling over his dripping blood and dying. But isn't it better not to die? If we're not dead after all this then we might wage new wars which might be better than this one. And maybe Yaaqub would come back then and leave Aristotle behind and bear the *feda'i* gun with us.

Face three: it was just after April 23, 1969.* The pools of blood then coating the streets of Beirut signaled the onset of the torrent of blood that was later to convulse the city. Salem came to the university and found that half the students had gone into class. He stood in the courtyard of the school and made a speech. It wasn't a speech so much as a stream of curses against the police, the state, and America. Then the school went on strike. A few fist-fights broke out and everyone went on his way. As Salem was stepping out of the gate on his way home, he discovered there was a car waiting for him which hauled him off to the police station. I sat, with scores of other students, in a dark room as insults were hurled at us.

—I'm thirsty, *effendi.***

But the *effendi* wouldn't answer.

—God keep you, *effendi*, please, a drink.

The *effendi* got a pitcher of water, stood it in front of the metal bars, told us to stand up and drink from behind the bars.

—Ya *effendi*, what's going on? Surely . . . this isn't Israel. What have we done?

The *effendi* took the pitcher away and no one drank. Then he came back with three bullyboys, unlocked the door and took us out one by one, lashed us brutally, kicking us around with his boots. We lay thrown to the ground then he climbed onto my body, trampled and trampled, to his

---

* The start of a seven-month-long cabinet crisis in Lebanon when there was only a caretaker government. This followed a period of mounting tension between the Lebanese state and the PLO.

** Originally a Turkish word meaning "mister," still used today in its slightly modified form to address officers, especially in the police force.

heart's content, and until the blood started oozing out of my ears. Then they grouped us in rows of three, the officer stood before us and made a speech about Lebanon and how we should love our country, then ordered us to chant "long live Lebanon." We chanted, left the police station, and wiped away the traces of our injuries. What we didn't realize then was that the war had begun. Then, it spread to Ghandour, to the killings.* Then it was ablaze and it stayed that way.

The triangle fits inside the circle. But we didn't know that the war had started. We thought it would just be a question of reordering the givens of the triangle, of modifying its premises. However, when the triangle blew up, the bloodshed was interminable. It went on until the whole circle collapsed. Every circle is bound to collapse, that is the rule; and when it does, the three faces of the triangle shatter. And we sit under the rain looking for new triangles.

I was all alone. The only horseman. Surrounded by the night with a woman saying she loved me and a circle waiting for me.

* * *

—But Bergis, we're here, not in Beirut or Barcelona or Madrid. Paris is a solid, stable city. Talking about civil war here is quite uncalled for. The National Assembly elections are due in a few months' time and the left's victory is not certain. Even if it is victorious, developments à la Chile are not inevitable. Giscard d'Estaing can dissolve the assembly, dollars will come pouring in to shore up the spirit of the Helsinki conference, the Socialists—half of whom are Zionists and the other half favorable to NATO—

---

* The name of the largest confectionary manufacturers in Lebanon whose workers were in the vanguard of the worker protest movement of the early '70s. During a peaceful demonstration in 1972, several of them were killed when the army opened fire on the demonstrators.

will be split and France will have averted a civil war. Of course, Paris will be destroyed eventually—like any other city—but not that quickly. Or at any rate, not by civil war. A world war is perhaps the only way to achieve such destruction.

But Bergis wouldn't answer, he just stood there in the middle of the subway passages, then led me to a big map of the metro routes hanging on the wall and started up his monologue. Look, look, he'd say.

—But why? Are you on the verge of bankruptcy or something?

—Not at all, quite the contrary. Haven't you seen the new restaurant?

Tomorrow you'll come and visit the restaurant.

—Are you feeling depressed? Do you want a divorce?

—Why are you asking me such silly questions? I'm a measured, civilized man, I'm a businessman.

—Then why are you chasing after a civil war?

—Me? Chasing after? No, no. I'm against civil wars. But I'm frightened. When I see what happened in Lebanon, I'm overcome with dread that similar devastation is going to engulf the world. And I'm frightened of devastation. Three times already I've started all over again, from scratch. The first time was in Vietnam and that was destroyed. Then I went to Algeria and opened up a shop for household appliances. I believed de Gaulle when he said we wouldn't leave Algeria. I really believed him. And expanded the business since we were staying. That whole war there didn't concern me: I was on good terms with the French as a French national; and on good terms with the NLF people as a Lebanese. Then de Gaulle went and left, he fled. Though in a reasonable way, this time; but he made me lose my business—and my mind. I abandoned the shop and came to Paris to start all over again from scratch. It seems things always lead nowhere in these damned times.

—And if there's a civil war, on whose side will you be?

—I won't be. I'm a practical man, a resilient Lebanese. My head belongs in my pocket. I put my mind in my pocket and let it lead the way. Be there civil war or a victory of the left, my head will lead me some place else. I'll go to Latin America. This time, however, not with nothing but with my fortune. I've got everything ready.

Poor Bergis. Standing before the metro board, gesticulating. Like the traffic policeman who insisted on doing his duty in Beirut: gunmen came and took his pistol; still, he stood in the middle of the street, signaling to the few cars that dared to move about; then it got to be he was signaling to the shells: he just stayed there, standing in the middle of the empty avenue signaling to anything until a shell hit him and he died.

—Look how this city intertwines inside this damned metro, it's crazy. Here, you come out in the Algerian immigrants' quarter. Here, the Champs-Elysées. Here, the Place de la Concorde. What would stop the inhabitants of those Arab neighborhoods from reaching the Place de la Concorde? Things are both open and interlocking, they can destroy one another at any time. Didn't I tell you? Civil war is inevitable. Tell me, tell me how the civil war started in Lebanon.

I didn't tell him. I was standing with her beside me. We came out at the Place de la Concorde and saw the sky. A vast square and above it the sky. The sky wasn't just an extension of the square, but a dome. Standing on the ground I could feel a dome above my head. Blue or gray or white. The cobblestones and vast open spaces for horse-drawn carriages. A piece of sky, a slice of earth and me in between. Look, she said, look at civilization! But I couldn't see any civilization, just vast open spaces and eyes. I don't know where this business of the eyes came from, all I could see were eyes and spaces and residues of sky.

— Look, she said. Look at the time-honored civilization.

But I saw neither time-honored nor modern civilization. Only forms of things bending. There was everything here: water, sky, her lovely face, the white stone. Everything dancing in white. There, a hospital sign. No, an ancient Egyptian obelisk. For, during Napoleon's Egyptian campaign, historians, writers, and philosophers accompanied the soldiers. The soldiers looted and the men of learning studied Egyptian antiquity. Then the men of learning discovered they too could loot. So they started stealing the priceless objects, the Pharaonic mummies. They stole despite the Pharaoh's curse; they weren't afraid. And now there's this pure white obelisk standing in the middle of one of the most beautiful squares in the world. We went up to it: there were all sorts of pictures and signatures on it. Egyptian birds flitting from place to place. Innumerable scenes: looking at them, you can see men and women in ancient Egyptian costumes, words flying from their mouths and nestling in the stone; between one man another, a woman carrying a picture of the Pharaoh-god or her newborn child who would emerge as the builder of the tombs.

— Look, the most beautiful obelisk in the world standing witness to the continuity of civilizations. Civilizations piling on one another like silt at the mouth of a river. The most magnificent ancient civilization standing at the center of the most magnificent modern civilization.

I couldn't quite grasp the meaning of those words. What I do know is that they stuck the boot into our heads in the name of something very similar. Don't you read the papers? she exclaimed. They brought the mummy of Rameses II all the way from Egypt so it could be treated in Paris. Fungus had started to grow on his forehead and bacteria to eat away his right hand. That's why they admitted him here, at the hospital laboratory. He'll be treated and then he'll go back to his country, duly honored and revered. Yet another sign of the continuity between civilizations.

I didn't understand. I stepped forward, looked at the obelisk and saw its tapered, black head. Just as I was about to express amazement at such a unique architectural achievement with its mingled evocations of color, I noticed the black moving. It wasn't just a color. It was an extraneous body which moved, hanging on the pinnacle of the Egyptian obelisk. Moving right then left, like a weathervane. I got closer. No use. To see, I've got to take a step back. As I did so, I saw a small black body, the body of a man wearing the double crown,* nodding and smiling at the people gathered round the obelisk to watch this king.

—What's this? A man at the top of an obelisk!

—I don't see anything, she said. Just a black speck and you call that a man.

—It's a real man, I'm sure. It's a real man sitting at the top of the obelisk, governing the square.

Maybe he is the city's new governor.

The new city governor looks like Rameses II. He comes over every morning from his shack in the lab, saluting the applauding crowds. Then he ties a rope round his waist, scales up the obelisk, and seats himself on top. So as to go on feeling he's a king.

The little man who leaves the hospital every morning walks slowly. He's a sick, frail man, with a slight stoop and short legs, who mumbles incomprehensible words. Some of them come up to him to kiss his hand but he never

* An allusion to the unity of Egypt under the Pharaohs, the double crown referring to Lower Egypt and Upper Egypt.

allows it. He's a busy man, in charge of governing a vast land. Although he doesn't understand these new usages in government, he does follow them. He has to scale up a tall obelisk as if he were one of the construction workers. Then he has to sit on something like a stake. There are different kinds, the king thinks to himself: the deadly kind that enters the flesh at the bottom of the spine and comes out at the neck; then, the disfiguring kind which is senseless except that it's used as a revenge: here, a naked or almost naked corpse is brought along and impaled; and then this new kind of stake. No, it's not a stake, the king thinks, it's the new throne.

The slight pain the king feels gradually recedes before the beauty of the square. He drops down from his throne every evening and walks down a long and winding road. He can deviate from his route somewhat, to please the public, but in the end he has to get to the hospital.

The king enters. His majesty the king, with his short build, habitual stoop, and modern clothes. He bows once more just in case his first bow wasn't seen by the entire public or maybe as an affirmation of his democratic humil- ity or for any other reason we happen to ignore — though his majesty doesn't ignore it. He knows everything. And like sovereigns like people, as my father says. While yet corrupt- ing them, kings are sovereign over our cities. For, "kings, when they enter a city, disorder it and make the mighty ones of its inhabitants abased," as Abu Ziad would say when we asked him what he thought of the current situation. Though Abu Ziad knows nothing about politics. He cares only for the little shop we used to go to, rifles slung across our shoulders, to buy what little food he sold, always giving thanks to the Lord. Then, when the rifles vanished and the customers disappeared and new customers came stomping in in their ugly boots, he took to cursing the times and their sovereigns and to repeating this favorite verse of his. And you had to listen were you buying for a thousand pounds' worth. Or else he wouldn't sell. The king bows, advances, the applause swells, the square shrinks. It shrinks until it is a small box. The obelisk grows, soars up until it is a stake. I run up to the king, I want to ask him a specific question. I want to ask him about the accuracy of newspaper reports that he is being treated for a fungus growing on his forehead and for bacteria eating away his hand.

—What's the real story, Your Majesty?

But his majesty doesn't answer. There's a cold wind blowing, it's a huge square and his majesty is in a hurry. He wants to get the ceremonial over with so he can get to work. Though she's beside me she doesn't see. Why can't this woman see my face and the fungus growing on it, and my hand with the bacteria eating it away? Why can she only see civilizations—as though civilizations were sacks of potatoes, all mixed up together, so that you can't differentiate between them? But she can't see and the king won't answer as the wind lashes against his frail body fluttering like a black cloth, an emblem of mourning in a square filling with white and the countless bows of men who have come from every continent.

I held her hand. She was flying across the square, and I loved her. But my body hurt. Things grow or they don't, but it's more complicated than that as I always like to say to avoid getting trapped into positions I reject or to die confident that my picture hangs on the wall. He looks like an octopus: a featherless king with his tiny face, his limbs growing and coiling around the Egyptian obelisk in order to grab my head and crush it, but I escape. I run in the middle of the square, it's surrounded by a long, thick wall. I can't do anything. I need a knife, to chop off the black extremities. I'm in the corner, my hand gripping a sharp blade. And the blood around my head is like a crown I don't want to shed. I'm the real king, I told her. But she doesn't understand. Why won't this woman understand? And why this wall? And this other king?

* * *

The rain drenching my head and clothes began to dry off. That stubborn man was still holding onto my arm, he wouldn't let me out of the subway passage. A stubborn man that Bergis Nohra. That's why his mouth was reeking of alcohol and it was driving me to the brink of despair. Still, in spite of everything, I'm willing to be convinced. I can be convinced that all cities are alike, and all squares too. But I cannot be convinced that women are all alike. The question is more complicated than that and needs to be completely re-examined. While we were destroying Beirut we thought we'd destroyed it. We'd run through the devastated squares and the buildings that had collapsed—or almost collapsed—convinced that we'd destroyed the city. In the end, we did destroy it but when they announced the war was over and published pictures of the terrible devastation that had been visited upon Beirut, we discovered that we hadn't destroyed it. We had made a few breaches in its ramparts but she wasn't destroyed. New wars are probably needed to do that. Nevertheless, all cities are alike, of that I'm convinced. Although I didn't know why they built squares in the middle of cities. To aerate them, my father said, so that the houses don't devour one another and fungus won't grow on the children's faces. But Jamal Pasha* saw otherwise. I remember that after the 1958 disturbances they arrested a man called al-Takmeel and pinned on him all the crimes that had been committed during the civil unrest. Then they told him to pretend he was mad. So he grew his

---

* Jamal Pasha, nicknamed 'the killer', was the Ottoman military governor of Lebanon who ordered the hanging of 33 nationalists in 1915–16.

beard and took to sitting around the prison saying he was God and sent the president of the republic letters preaching his new faith and proclaiming his innocence of the crimes attributed to him. He was pretty convincing: it was clear that the lawyer who'd persuaded him to become mad wrote these nice evangelizing letters. Things didn't go as planned, however. The ropes had to be persuaded and ropes aren't easily convinced. So they hanged him. In front of the gallows, Takmeel was no longer mad. He confessed and sought forgiveness. I'm not the only criminal, he said, the real criminal is still in his house or in his street or in another city. Although the hangman appeared convinced that day, there wasn't any time, so he hanged him. The policemen's consciences were eased; now they could go back to their customary nice duties.

All squares are alike. There are white squares and green squares and gray squares. I prefer white squares, she said.

—But they look like hospitals and smell of a combination of medicine and plasma.

—No, they are the squares of kings.

—But I hate kings, I prefer gray squares. In gray squares, there are prisons and in prison there is rest. There are times when prisons are necessary perhaps: I can rest a little bit there and forget my worries, because prisons generate their own, persuasive worries.

All squares are alike. Even in green squares where there's grass and flowers and water, you'll either find a rope dangling or a king, or a stake which looks like complicated artistic things. On closer inspection, you realize that it's just a very ordinary stake.

The square was empty. The sounds were the voices of hawkers who'd awakened early and carried their loads of fruits and vegetables to the various neighborhoods so that the day might start and things proceed as they should. Like that, in spite of everything, things could go on being the way they should. Actually, to be precise, there were also the sounds of garbage trucks with their load of workers making the rounds of the refined residential quarters to prevent the spread of disease. And still a few pale lights flickering like early morning lights. Standing in the square, with her holding my hand and a short, fat man standing in front of me, his neck thick as a wild boar's, slightly stooped, clutching a scroll covered in writing of all sorts of letters. Standing exactly opposite me, looking me in the eye. Next to the man, a long rope dangling down as though descended from the sky. The man came up to me and began to read from the scroll he was clutching. I didn't understand a thing, looked at her. Her face dilated, whitening. It seemed she understood the terrible words the man was uttering.

—What's he saying?

—What he's saying is not important. What's important is that what's said in books will come true.

—But what's said in books?

—They've written a lot of things in books. And they'll come true. As for us, we neither like books nor reading them. What's written in them is of no concern to us because we know exactly what the fate of books is. Our professor knows it too. I met him in the street as the shells flew about the sky over the city. I didn't recognize him to begin with. He looked wasted, crushed. His mouth pulled slightly to the right, a little more than necessary. Then I realized he must have been ill and it had twisted his lower jaw.

I went to the university, he said, saw unbelievable things. Why did they do that? It's a crime against future generations. Plundered the place, they have, taking chairs, tables, carpets, blackboards, chalk, the lot. Never mind, those things can always be replaced. But the library. Do you know what they did to it? If only they'd looted it, one could say that they were getting something out of the books at least. I went to the library and found the books—simply torn. A million pounds' worth of books torn to shreds, trampled, strewn all over the place, the garden, the window sills. I'm on their side, with their cause, but what is the fault of the books!

I pacified him somewhat and went on my way.

He was suffocatingly self-assured and I didn't understand his utterances. He came closer. I was standing with my back to a thick, impenetrable wall. He put his mouth right up to my face so that I felt he was about to swallow me. I tried stepping back but couldn't. Then he began to spray spittle as he read faster and faster, the spray coming quicker and quicker at my face until I screamed for him to stop. But he just went on, driven like a blind, uncomprehending machine. Then, slowly, under this foul-smelling spray, it began to dawn on me: he seemed to be speaking about dangerous things, multiple sentences, executions, hangings.

But the man with a neck thick as a boar's went on as if hearing nothing or, rather, as if he didn't want to hear. It would seem that the major part of his job consists in not listening to what the defendants have to say. Once in a while, one of them is pretty convincing and that's a threat to the thick-necked man's job. He's the head of a large household, after all, he's got to live and he knows of no other job that pays as well even though all the neighbors think it's a revolting thing to do. However, as far as he can see, all professions are revolting, they're all alike, and you can't beat drinking at the fountainhead. That's why he sticks to this job. He would not stop. Reading the scroll, articulating every sound. He couldn't care one way or another about the contents. What matters is the job. In a few moments, this man must be hanged. The actual hanging operation doesn't take very long, a few minutes to listen to the statement of the accused, then a few more minutes to carry out his last wish. They usually ask for a cigarette and smoke it extremely slowly. But however slowly you smoke a cigarette—and especially an American cigarette—it is quickly finished. Then starts the real work—which doesn't take very long if he's prepared the rope properly. Whereupon, the job's over when he scales up the man's legs and pulls down hard so he doesn't suffer too much. The thing he hates most about this job is reading out the scroll. In the past, a magistrate was brought over to read out the sentence. But now he has to do it. He knows it's not legal, that the verdict hasn't been handed down by a legal body. But he doesn't care, legal bodies or not, they're all the same. And everything leads to one result and that is the continuation of his job.

The man stepped forward, wearing the customary white robe. The square was green, the sky gray. He didn't request anything, not even that the foul-smelling spray be wiped off his face.

—A cigarette?

He didn't answer. Simply shook his head.

—Would you like anything?

He didn't answer. Simply shook his head.

—What is your bequest?

He didn't answer. Simply shook his head.

What is this new kind of man, thought the thick-necked man. Still, in the end, before the rope, they're all the same: they tremble and begin to rattle off verses and incantations, begging forgiveness and crying. The man in the white robe advanced. He wasn't trembling. His right foot trembled just a little maybe. But that isn't important. He came forward, there were traces of burns on his face and water bled from his ears. He didn't say anything, went up the steps, put his head through the noose, his body a little bent, trembling slightly. But he went up with a firm step. He could go no farther. He held him up. Lights colored the sky and his body was as a dough of constantly changing tints. He didn't fall. She took him. His body quivered as though feverish. Then he fell. And it was a very long way. That is the point. The long way, and the long square, and the long rope. But the king was short and he trembled. The obelisk was long. What's said in books will come true, she said.

But books are far away and it's a very long way. Ropes are more important than books, I answered.

We were walking, her hand in mine, the sadness blowing across the face of the city buffeting our faces. The man they hanged was sad. Next time, we shouldn't content ourselves with stealing the rope, we should break it; next time, we shouldn't content ourselves with overrunning the squares and the buildings, we should destroy them. The essential thing, though, is that there should be a next time.

— Didn't I tell you? All squares look alike. All cities with tunnels boring through them will be destroyed. Bergis was looking completely haggard now, beginning to slither away inside his clothes until nothing was left of him but clothes in motion, the sweat streaming out of them. He'd started to think about the Foreign Legion again. The Foreign Legion is just a temporary solution, but it's better than nothing. Clothes in motion and the gesticulations no longer meaning much. The Foreign Legion is the only solution. It's better than nothing. It may become everything.

I left him and ran for the metro. I didn't turn to look back, just ran fast. She may still be waiting for me.

Elias
KHOURY

Elias Khoury is a lecturer at the American University of Beirut and the cultural editor of the daily *al-Safir*. He has taught at the Lebanese University in Beirut and, in the United States, at Columbia University. Khoury has published book-length works in various genres, including novels, critical essays, and short stories, and he is a frequent contributor to literary and cultural journals in the Arab world, including *Mawaqif Quarterly* and *al-Adab*. His novels, published in Arabic, include *White Faces* (1981), *City Gates* (1981), and *The Travel of Little Ghandi* (1989). *Little Mountain*, his second novel, was published in Beirut in 1977.

Maia Tabet is a free-lance translator and editor. She earned her degree in political science and philosophy at the American University of Beirut in 1980. She has worked in Beirut as an instructor at the American Language Center, as a writer-reporter for several Lebanese magazines and newspapers, and, most recently, as an administrator for Oxfam. She is co-editor of a book on Afro-Arab relations.

Edward W. Said is Parr Professor of English and Comparative Literature at Columbia University. He is the author of *Orientalism* (nominated for the National Book Critic's Circle Award), *The Question of Palestine*, *Covering Islam*, *The World, the Text, and the Critic*, and *After the Last Sky: Palestinian Lives*.